GUNS OF MIST RIVER

GUNS OF MIST RIVER

Jackson Cole

Chivers Press • **G.K. Hall & Co.**
Bath, England **Thorndike, Maine USA**

This Large Print edition is published by Chivers Press, England, and by G.K. Hall & Co., USA.

Published in 1999 in the U.K. by arrangement with Golden West Literary Agency.

Published in 1999 in the U.S. by arrangement with Golden West Literary Agency.

U.K. Hardcover   ISBN 0-7540-3852-1   (Chivers Large Print)
U.K. Softcover   ISBN 0-7540-3853-X   (Camden Large Print)
U.S. Softcover   ISBN 0-7838-8648-9   (Nightingale Series Edition)

The text of this Large Print edition is unabridged.
Other aspects of the book may vary from the original edition.

Set in 16 pt. New Times Roman.

Printed in Great Britain on acid-free paper.

British Library Cataloguing in Publication Data available

Library of Congress Cataloging-in-Publication Data

Cole, Jackson.
    Guns of Mist River : a Texas Ranger novel / Jackson Cole.
       p.   cm.
    ISBN 0-7838-8648-9 (lg. print : sc : alk. paper)
    1. Texas Rangers—Fiction. 2. Large type books. I. Title.
    [PS3505.O2685G86   1999]
    813'.54—dc21   99–29287

CHAPTER ONE

CLOUD OF DUST

When Jim Hatfield first saw the herd, it was but a tawny dust cloud rising slowly against the distant skyline. A cloud that rolled steadily westward, its golden mist swirling upward to dissipate in the blue of the Texas sky.

From where Hatfield sat on his great golden horse, a long slope tumbled steeply downward to the level rangeland beyond. Still farther beyond was Mist River, winding and shining in the sun, cleaving the green and amethyst prairie that dimmed eastward into the distances.

To the south of the ridge crest, Mist River abandoned its low though steep banks and dived into the dark mouth of a towering-walled canyon. The rimrock of the canyon was a torn and jagged saw-edge of black stone mottled with white and banded with scarlet and russet and yellow. The hills whose frowning battlements the canyons pierced, looked like great irregular blocks of granite that had been hurled helter-skelter by Titans at play.

Eastward from the crest of the ridge ran a trail, winding down the long slope to slice off at the river's brink and flow on wearily beyond

1

its gleaming waters. Following the general direction of this trail was the approaching dust cloud. Hatfield could vision the churning hoofs beating its surface into the rising fog that glittered in the sunshine.

Hatfield eyed the approaching herd, still invisible under the dust cloud, with the disapproval of an experienced cattleman.

'No sense in shoving cows along like that, especially in warm weather,' he remarked to Goldy, his horse. 'Runs the fat off 'em. That owner will find himself pounds light per critter when he gets them to the pens. He'd better be saving their wind for this sag and the rough country beyond. Reckon he's headed for the railroad town we passed through ten miles to the west.'

Another ten minutes and the bouncing dots that were the individual animals were plainly visible under the dust cloud. Hatfield saw a number of horsemen shoving the herd along. All were behind the moving cows.

'Nobody at point or swing,' he mused thoughtfully. 'Everybody riding drag. Well, there isn't much chance for them to turn with the trail running straight across the range, so nobody's needed along the sides of the bunch, at that. And that's always the system when a man is in a hurry. But I still can't figure why he's got such a hustle on. That is, unless—'

His long green eyes narrowed slightly with thought. Instinctively, his slender, bronzed

2

hands dropped to the butts of the heavy black guns that sagged from the double cartridge belts encircling his lean waist. He loosened the long Colts in their carefully worked and oiled cut-out holsters. After all, a hustling herd might be shoved along by somebody under whose name their brand was *not* registered.

'Though how anybody could wideloop a herd in this direction is more than I can make out,' he decided. 'No turning aside in the hills west of here, and the trail runs right through that railroad town.'

Thoughtfully he eyed the approaching cows. They were less than a mile from the river bank now, and coming along at a great rate.

At undiminished speed the herd thundered to the river's brink. Behind the lumbering cows, the horsemen waved slickers and hats, slapping the frantic beefs across their rumps. Hatfield could almost hear the shouts and whoops. He saw the riders fan out to one side, race along the herd, veering it from the trail and to the left. Then they fell back and charged in a strung-out line at the rear.

The cows reached the edge of the perpendicular bank, bawling and bleating. Over the lip went the leaders, shoved ahead by the charging mass behind. The water foamed up in silvery spray as the heavy bodies crashed its surface. In scant minutes the stream was dotted with brown heads and heaving backs. Then the current caught the swimming animals

3

and swept them downstream. One after another they vanished from sight into the dark mouth of the canyon.

When the last cow was in the stream, the horsemen swerved their mounts and diagonaled south by east across the prairie. They did not back-track by way of the trail.

And with good reason. Sitting his horse on the ridge crest, too far away to hope to take part in the hectic activity, even had he desired, Hatfield saw the next act of the peculiar drama.

A second dust cloud had for some time been rising in the east. Now Hatfield saw a string of bouncing dots swerve from the trail and stream southward, apparently bent on intercepting the speeding horsemen who had shoved the herd into the river. At a long slant the two bodies of riders drew together, toward the apex of a triangle that would be the curve of the rangeland around the jagged eastern approaches of the hills that flanked the canyon.

Tense with interest, Hatfield watched the race. He saw white puffs mushroom from the ranks of the men to the north. The next instant answering puffs stained the air to the south.

The men to the south reached the curve of the hill slopes first, veered around it and disappeared from view. The pursuers, still shooting, galloped after them to vanish from sight in turn.

Hatfield relaxed. He shook his head. The thing was beyond words. It just naturally didn't make sense.

'What in blazes is the meaning of all this?' he demanded of himself at length. 'Why should some riders shove a big bunch of cows into the river to drown in that canyon? I've a notion the cows belonged to the second bunch that came along gunning for the first ones. They seemed to be plenty riled, all right.' He kept peering ahead for another sight of them.

'Wonder if they caught up with the hellions? Don't think so, though. Those riders in front had a good head start when they swerved around the hills. They'll likely get in the clear as soon as it is dark, and that isn't far off. What is going on around here, anyhow? Looks to me as if it'll stand being looked into.'

For another thoughtful space he sat his horse on the ridge crest, a striking figure outlined against the blaze of the western sky.

A tall man, much more than six feet, broad of shoulder, deep of chest, and slim of waist and hips, Hatfield's girth matched his height. His face was deeply bronzed and lean. The upward quirking of the corners of his rather wide mouth somewhat modified the tinge of fierceness evinced by the prominent high-bridged nose and the low powerful chin. The hair showing beneath his pushed back 'JB' was thick, and midnight black. The arresting face was dominated by long, black-lashed eyes of a peculiar shade of green beneath heavy black brows.

With a word, he sent his great golden sorrel, appropriately named Goldy, down the slope at a fast pace. Reaching the river, he found that the trail led to a ford.

The water there hardly came to Goldy's knees. But the current ran swiftly, swirling the water around the sorrel's legs and throwing up little flickers of foam.

Hatfield glanced toward the canyon mouth into which the cattle had disappeared, and shook his head.

'Poor critters never had a chance,' he muttered. 'Must run like a millrace in there, and more than likely there are rapids farther along. One mighty mean thing to do to a bunch of cows. Those fellows who shoved them in must be plenty snake-blooded.' A flash of anger showed in his green eyes.

'Yes, sir,' he mumbled, 'I reckon it's a salty country all right. Well, Goldy, that's what Captain McDowell said it was when he headed us over this way.'

For several miles, to a little past the point where Hatfield had first noticed the dust cloud boiling into the sky the trail traversed the level rangeland, with luxuriant grass the sole vegetation.

Then it wound between groves and thickets and finally entered a considerable belt of chaparral. And here Hatfield found grisly evidence that the country he had reached was salty.

Where the growth of the chaparral began, the trail forked, the lesser branch veering east with a slight southerly trend. The more traveled track continued north east. Pulling Goldy to a halt, Hatfield considered the two forks. He rolled a cigarette with the fingers of one hand and smoked thoughtfully as his gaze roamed from one direction to the other.

'Now,' he remarked to the sorrel who pricked up his ears, 'I've an idea this left-hand track probably heads for that town we were told about. I reckon we might as well amble along that way. Be dark before long and we could both stand a little nourishment. You've been doing pretty well, you old grass burner, but I'm not Nebuchadnezzar. I can't live on grass. That requires a special dispensation of Providence and is plumb out for the ordinary digestive organs. My stomach just isn't built that way. Broiled steak or ham and eggs are more my style. All right, Goldy, let's get started.'

Carefully he pinched out his cigarette butt and cast it aside. Then he sent Goldy along the north fork of the trail.

For perhaps a quarter of a mile he rode through the chaparral, which was steadily growing shadowy with oncoming night. Then with a sharp exclamation, he abruptly jerked Goldy to a halt.

7

At the edge of the growth stood a tall tree, one great branch stretching across the track. And from this branch, a rope around his neck, dangled the body of a man.

Hatfield's scalp prickled. He felt the palms of his hand moisten. A dead man is seldom a pretty sight, a hanged man, never.

Hatfield moved Goldy closer and looked over the body with care. He noted several surprising things about the dead man, and was about to dismount for an even more thorough inspection when Goldy suddenly pricked up his ears.

Hatfield stopped short and listened.

From somewhere ahead sounded the patter of hoofs of several horses.

Hatfield quickly backed Goldy into the brush until both he and his mount could not be seen from the trail. This man, Jim Hatfield, whom a stern old Lieutenant of Texas Rangers had named the 'Lone Wolf,' seldom missed any bets. He knew that it was not good judgment for a stranger in any section of country to be found beside a slain man.

Also, there was no telling who the approaching horseman might be. Not knowing themselves observed, they might reveal some valuable information.

Hardly had Hatfield reached his place of concealment when his keen ears detected more sounds, these from the south. Hoof beats again approaching.

'This is getting interesting,' he told himself. He slid from the saddle and moved silently to where he could peer through the fringe of growth.

Around the bend to the north bulged six or seven horsemen. Instantly they sighted the dangling body and jerked their mounts to a halt, with a volley of exclamations.

One rider, a lanky, grizzled old man with a bristling mustache rode forward a pace.

'Damn!' he swore. 'Clem Buster of the Bradded R!'

His companions rode forward, cursing. And around the bend to the south swept another band of horsemen, nearly a dozen. They also jerked their horses to a halt and sat staring.

Riding slightly in advance of the others of this group was a short, broad, strongly built man with long, powerful looking arms. He was an ugly man with a big nose covered with excresences, thick lips, a long, blue chin and high cheek-bones. His black eyes glinted in the shadow of his low-drawn hat brim. He peered with out-thrust neck at the swinging body. His face darkened with anger and his gaze flickered to the horsemen clustered near the death tree.

'You blasted to blazes killin' sidewinders!' he roared.

Instantly the men in both groups were clutching weapons. But before one of them could clear leather, a voice rolled in thunder from the growth that flanked the trail:

'Hold it! You're covered! Elevate, pronto!'

CHAPTER TWO

RANGE WAR

The belligerent horsemen jerked as if touched by hot irons.

'Elevate!' the voice from the brush repeated, in tones that demanded obedience. An ominous double clicking of drawn-back gun hammers served to emphasize the command.

Muttering curses, the riders obeyed, glaring at the shadowy growth.

Hatfield stepped into view, a long-barreled gun in each hand clamped against his hips, the black muzzles flaring out to cover both groups.

'Careful, boys,' the grizzled old man instantly cautioned. 'A man who fans his irons out sideways like that don't miss.' He raised his voice. 'Who the devil are you,' he demanded, 'and what do you want?'

Hatfield gave his name.

'Don't want anything,' he said then, 'except to keep you men from making darn fools of yourselves and going in for some needless gunning. I happened to get here before either of you, and that man was hanging there then.

So don't go off half-cocked and accuse one another of stringing him up till you know what you're talking about.'

The old man in the lead of the first group leaned forward, peering at Hatfield. 'You mean that?'

'You heard me say it.'

The oldster, his hands stiffly above his head, turned to gaze to the big leader of the opposing group.

'Hear that, Rawlins?' he said. 'I believe this man is tellin' the truth.'

'Reckon he is,' the rider called Rawlins admitted grudgingly, his voice a deep lion's growl. 'But I would not put it past you devils doin' it, if you got the chance, Skelton.'

'Listen, you!' bawled the oldster, his mustache bristling in his scarlet face. 'Some day you'll go too dad-blamed far!'

'I'll go all the way when I do,' the stocky rider instantly countered. 'I want to tell you . . .'

'Hold it!' Hatfield thundered. 'I don't know what this is all about, but it sure sounds loco to me. Now listen!' He jerked his right-hand gun toward the old man. 'You fellows turn about and hightail it back the way you come. Don't stop in a hurry, either. These hoglegs carry quite a ways, and I've got good ears. And they aren't all . . . Goldy!'

There was a crackling in the brush and the great sorrel moved into view and halted directly behind his rider.

11

'That saddle gun there in the boot is point-blank up to three hundred yards, and sighted for fifteen hundred,' Hatfield remarked with meaning. 'Get going. You other fellows stay put.'

'You're pullin' this mighty high-handed,' the old man growled.

But just the same, his face showed relief.

'Get going,' Hatfield repeated. 'Let your hands down easy, and hightail.'

The first group of horsemen obeyed. Hatfield noted grins flickering across the faces of several of the young cowhands who rode with the old man, Skelton. The hoofs clicked out of sight and kept on clicking until they faded into the distance.

'Say, mister,' the big-nosed Rawlins said plaintively, 'can't we put our hands down? This is gettin' mighty uncomfortable. Give you my word we won't try anything.'

Hatfield shot him a keen glance. 'Your word is good enough for me,' he said, and holstered his guns.

Rawlins lowered his hands with a sigh of relief. A grin widened his thick lips, revealing strong, crooked teeth that were glistening white. He nodded to the Lone Wolf.

'I'll say much obliged for everybody,' he remarked. 'If it wasn't for you, some of us wouldn't be in a position to say anything. Raines Skelton and his bunch may be snake-blooded, but they're plenty salty.'

12

Hatfield nodded. He had already arrived at the same conclusion concerning the saltiness of Skelton and his riders. He reserved judgment on the first part of what Rawlins had said.

'You know the man there on the tree?' he asked.

Rawlins' face darkened. 'It's Clem Buster, one of my hands,' he said. 'You sure that Raines and his side winders weren't holed up just around the bend when you got here?'

'I gather you mean they had just cashed in this puncher,' Hatfield interpreted. 'Well, if they did, they sure put in a lot of time around that bend. Besides, this poor cowhand didn't die by hanging.'

'What! He's got a rope around his neck, ain't he? And he sure ain't standing on anything but air.'

'That's right,' Hatfield admitted, 'but take a look at the rope. You'll notice the flesh of his neck isn't swollen around it. And see that stain on the left breast of his shirt? And if you look real close, you'll see there's a hole in the middle of the stain. That stain is dried blood. The poor fellow was shot to death—drilled dead center—several hours ago. His dead body was hanged.'

With a sharp exclamation, Rawlins slid from his hull and strode forward.

'I'll be plumb blasted, you're right!' he swore.

He reached out gingerly and touched the dead man's leg.

'Uh-huh, stiff already,' he growled. He fingered his long chin, with thick, stubby fingers, plainly at a loss.

'And if you're able to backtrack the moves of Skelton and his bunch,' Hatfield went on, 'you may be able to establish for sure that they couldn't have had anything to do with the killing and hanging.'

Rawlins continued to finger his chin. 'Town isn't more than twenty minutes ride, by the trail,' he observed, as if communing with himself. 'Chances are Skelton left town and headed back to his spread, which is by way of the east fork of the trail, back a little ways. If we find out he was in town for quite a spell, as I reckon he would be, that would put him and his bunch in the clear all right. That is, the bunch he had with him. Plenty more Forked S hands than the ones you saw, Hatfield. We're just back from tryin' to run down some of them that lifted a herd off my Bradded R spread. They got into the hills before we could drop a loop on 'em, and gave us the slip.'

'Did they get the cows into the hills, too?' Hatfield asked casually.

Rawlins swore viciously. 'No!' he said. 'They did with the cows what they've done before. Shoved 'em into Mist River to drown. They're not wideloopers—got plenty beefs of their own. Just plumb ornery.'

14

'Shoved 'em in the river to drown, eh?' Hatfield repeated. 'Doesn't seem to make sense.'

'No?' Rawlins commented sarcastically. 'Well, it'll make more sense to you when you learn somethin' of what's goin' on in this part of the country. Clean a man's spread of cows and he's out of business, ain't he?'

'Usually,' Hatfield admitted, 'unless he can get more cows.'

'Cows cost money, and if you haven't got it, you don't get 'em, that is without a slick iron and a wide loop,' Rawlins growled. 'Skelton and his riders know that. They aim to run me off the range, that's all.'

'Why?' Hatfield asked.

'Because I'm not an old-timer here and they don't like new people coming in,' Rawlins replied. 'They've been here since Noah shoved the first cow out of the Ark. Been runnin' things their way so long they think they own this whole end of the state. They're plumb ornery, like I said, and won't stop at anythin'.'

He made a significant gesture toward the dangling body.

Hatfield nodded. He was not ready to comment until he learned more.

'Reckon we might as well ride to town,' Rawlins decided, and at a murmur from his men he shook his head. 'No, boys, we won't cut poor Buster down. Leave him for the sheriff and the coroner to see. Not that it'll do

15

him or us any good. The sheriff is tight-looped with Skelton. Come on, let's go.'

He mounted his horse and gathered up the reins. Hatfield would have preferred less chance of a meeting in town between the two outfits, but he couldn't tell the people of the range where and how to ride on an open trail.

'I'll ride along with you, if you don't mind,' he said to Rawlins. 'Feel the need of a good meal.'

'Sure, come along,' Rawlins said. 'Plenty of good eatin' places in Crater. I suppose the Deuces Up is about as good as any. They sell fairly good liquor there, too, and the games are as straight as any.'

As they rode the trail, Hatfield at Rawlins' stirrup, the Lone Wolf covertly studied the Bradded R owner. Rawlins had the look of being a hard man. His tight jaw and the quick glitter of his black eyes said so unmistakably. He looked intelligent, too.

'And stubborn as a blue-nosed mule,' Hatfield decided.

The Bradded R riders, a silent bunch, also had the appearance of being cold propositions. Hatfield knew that the taciturn riders were giving him a careful once-over and arriving at conclusions. He hoped that an alibi would be speedily proved, in town, for Skelton and his bunch. Otherwise the thought might come to some of these efficient-looking hands that he, Hatfield, might be in cahoots with Skelton and planted in the brush to provide an alibi for the Forked S outfit when they heard the approach of the Bradded R men, who outnumbered them two to one.

The sun had set before they reached the cow and mining town of Crater. Through the deepening blue dusk, the lights of Crater were yellow stars against a sky of shadows. They outlined to squares and rectangles of saffron as the horses' irons beat the dust of the crooked main street. At corners, lanterns hung on poles added their flicker of illumination to the golden bars streaming through windows or over the swinging doors of the saloons.

Boot heels drummed the board sidewalks. There was a babble of talk, a bawling of song, the thrum of guitars, the whine of fiddles, the tapping of feet on dance floors. The clink of bottle necks on glasses, the rattle and whir of roulette wheels and the cheerful clink of gold pieces on the 'mahogany' provided sprightly overtones to the other sounds of revelry.

'Looks to be quite a town,' Hatfield commented to Rawlins.

'Uh-huh, she is,' the cowman agreed. 'Smells little strong of whisky, tobacco, and general ruckus raisin'. Good chance of sniffin' powder smoke most any night, too . . .' There's the Deuces Up right ahead. We'll stop off there for a spell. You might as well, too, if you want to eat.'

'Want to find a place for my horse, first,'

Hatfield said.

'Right around this corner, here,' Rawlins replied. 'Good stable. I'll lead you to it. We'll hitch our jugheads at the rack, because we'll be ridin' on to the spread before long ...' Go ahead, boys, while I show Hatfield the stable. Be with you in a minute.'

Rawlins walked on with Hatfield, and they turned into an alley. 'Aimin' to coil your twine hereabouts for a spell?' the rancher asked.

'Depends,' Hatfield replied. 'Looks like an interesting part of country.'

'I reckon some folks might find a rattlesnake den interestin',' Rawlins commented disgustedly. 'No accountin' for tastes. It is good cow country, though, and the mines in the hills to the southeast are puttin' plenty of money into them, and that makes things lively. If you're lookin' for a job of ridin', I'll talk to you later. Here's the stable.'

After obtaining suitable quarters for Goldy, and a room over the stalls for Hatfield, they repaired to the saloon Rawlins recommended. Hatfield at once sought out a table and ordered a meal. Rawlins went to the bar, and engaged the bartender in conversation. Then he sauntered over to Hatfield's table.

'You were right, Hatfield,' he said. 'Skelton and his bunch were in town all afternoon. They couldn't have had anything to do with what happened down the trail, or with wideloopin' and drownin' my cows, either. But there's

18

about thirty more wild-eyed punchers on the Forked S, so it don't mean much. There were plenty of 'em loose to do for Buster.'

'Any idea where Buster was this afternoon?' Hatfield asked.

'He was supposed to be on my southwest pasture, where the cows were run from,' Rawlins replied. 'He must have spotted the rustlers there and they did for him. What puzzles me is why in blazes did they pack him over to that thicket and string him up. Just plain meanness, I reckon.'

Hatfield was ready to agree that, on the surface at least, the thing didn't make sense. But he felt certain that the hanging was not a mere whim on the part of the men who killed Buster. He was convinced that there was a motive, doubtless a subtle and sinister one, back of the apparently wanton act.

'I'm goin' to look up the sheriff and tell him what happened,' Rawlins announced. 'Will you be here when I get back?' Hatfield nodded, and began eating.

CHAPTER THREE

A LINE ON FOLKS

Rawlins was back soon. With him was a rotund, jovial-looking individual who was introduced as John Dwyer, the sheriff of the county.

Sheriff Dwyer was serious enough, however, when he questioned Hatfield about his finding of Clem Buster's body. He shook his head sadly and there was a worried look in his faded blue eyes.

'Don't know what the country's comin' to,' he said. 'Gettin' worse all the time. There's been the devil to pay around here for the past six months. Never used to be that way.'

Hatfield saw Rawlins' thick lips tighten a little, but the Bradded R owner made no remark.

'I'll drive down there with a buckboard the first thing in the morning,' announced the sheriff. 'I'll take Doc Cooper, the coroner, with me. We'll bring Buster's body back. Doc will want to hold an inquest.'

'And bring in a verdict sayin' Buster met his death at the hands of parties unknown, like they said about my nighthawk, Turner, who was cashed in when the herd was run off my east range last month,' Rawlins commented sarcastically.

The sheriff flushed slightly. 'What else could Doc do?' he asked. 'Nobody saw Turner killed, any more'n they saw what happened to Buster. That is, nobody we know anything about.'

'Looks like somebody might try to find out something about somebody,' Rawlins grunted.

'That's unjust, Bert, and you know it,' the

20

sheriff said quietly.

'Well, maybe it is,' Rawlins grudgingly admitted, 'but you can't blame me for gettin' a little riled. Remember, I've lost hundreds of cows and two top hands in the past three months.'

'Skelton has lost cows, and so have other folks,' said the sheriff.

'That's what *he* says,' growled Rawlins.

'He has as much right to be believed as you have,' defended Dwyer.

Rawlins shoved his hat back and scratched his bristling red head.

'Looks like we ain't gettin' nowhere,' he said. 'I'm headin' back to the spread. Skelton and his bunch are in town and there's no sense in buckin' into trouble. Which is liable to happen if everybody gets liquored up.'

'That's showin' good sense,' the sheriff agreed in relieved tones. 'You'll be in town tomorrow, of course?'

'Uh-huh,' Rawlins replied. 'See you tomorrow, Hatfield. You'll be here, all right?'

'We'll want him at the inquest,' said the sheriff. He glanced questioningly at Hatfield. The Lone Wolf nodded.

Rawlins rose to his feet. The sheriff also prepared to depart. They left the saloon together.

Shortly after Hatfield finished eating and was enjoying a leisurely cigarette, old Raines Skelton stalked in. He glanced about, met

21

Hatfield's eyes, and frowned. He hesitated, apparently undecided as to just what course to pursue.

Hatfield smiled, his even teeth flashing startlingly white in his bronzed face, his green eyes crinkling at the corners, making his stern face friendly. Skelton tried to glower, but grinned instead. He walked over to Hatfield's table and plumped into a chair.

'Well,' he growled truculently, 'did you sign up with Bert Rawlins?'

Hatfield's smile broadened. 'I don't recall him asking me to,' he replied.

'Well,' Skelton growled again, 'he must be slippin'. Always makes it a point to hire every gun-slinger that happens along. Maybe you don't talk as salty as you looked to be out there on the trail, or he wouldn't have missed the bet. You thinkin' of staying a while on this range?'

'Depends,' Hatfield told him. 'I'm not anxious to take sides in a local ruckus I don't know anything about, if that's what you're getting at.'

'Then in that case you'd better sign up with Pres Morton and the Bar M,' Skelton snorted. 'He's about the only rancher hereabouts, except old Tol Truxton of the Lucky Seven, that hasn't taken a hand in this row. Pres says he don't see why folks can't get along together, no matter who they are or where they come from.'

'Sounds like good sense,' Hatfield replied. 'Just why are you on the prod against Rawlins?'

'This range was plumb peaceful till he showed up here, about six months back,' Skelton retorted.

'Meaning you think he's responsible for what's been happening?'

'Well,' Skelton replied belligerently, 'it's mighty funny, when we hadn't had any rustlin' or robbin' or killin' for a long spell and then they begin right after he comes here and takes over the Bradded R. I've been losin' cows, plenty, and so have other folks.'

'Rawlins says he's been losing cows, too,' Hatfield countered. 'Had them shoved in the river and drowned, like a bunch today he told me about. And he seems to know what he's talking about, on that score, anyhow.'

'You mean to say you believe that Rawlins really lost cows that way?' Skelton demanded incredulously.

'That's just what I mean,' Hatfield replied quietly. 'In fact, I know somebody lost cows that way today. I saw it happen.'

Old Raines Skelton stared. He shook his grizzled head. 'You talk like you're lyin', but you look like you're not,' he growled.

Hatfield did not resent the way the thing was said, understanding that Skelton was paying him a compliment.

'I was on the crest of the ridge west of the

river and saw it,' he explained. 'I was too far away to spot brands or faces, but I saw a bunch of riders shove the cows into the water, then hightail south and east around the hills. Another bunch galloped out of the brush to the north and chased 'em out of sight. According to what Rawlins told me, he and his men were that other bunch.'

'Looks that way,' Skelton admitted, a worried expression shadowing his face. 'Well, nobody can accuse me of bein' in on that. I was here in town all afternoon.'

'I understand you have quite a few men riding for you,' Hatfield remarked.

'Meanin' you think some of my boys might have been in on that?'

'I'm not saying anything like that,' Hatfield replied, 'but I do know that sometimes members of an outfit on the prod against another outfit get out of hand and do things on their own.'

'There's truth in that,' Skelton admitted gloomily. His face hardened. 'I know the boys are worked up against Rawlins and his hands, but if I find that anybody workin' for me is responsible for drownin' a lot of poor beef critters, there'll be a housecleanin' on the Forked S that'll make an old maids' home in springtime look plumb mild!' He hastened to add: 'Not that I believe there is. I know my boys, and nobody'll make me believe any of 'em would do a thing like that. I—'

He broke off to wave to a man who had just entered the room, slapping the dust from his hat against his overalled leg.

'Here comes Pres Morton, now,' Skelton said. 'Set down and take a load off your feet, Pres, and meet Jim Hatfield, who just got in town.'

Morton acknowledged the introduction, and sat down. He was a well-set-up man of slightly above medium height with powerful-looking shoulders. His lips were peculiarly thin and straight. His face was rather broad across the cheek-bones, which were low. His eyes were clear gray and unwinking, his hair dark and inclined to curl. He had a soft, low voice, and spoke like a man of some education.

Morton listened attentively as Skelton regaled him with an account of the day's happenings. He shook his head when the rancher had finished.

'You and Rawlins are headed for big trouble,' he said. 'You've got the makings of another Graham-Tewksbury war here. I know you have most of the cowmen hereabouts back of you, but Rawlins has about twenty salty hands riding for him, and he isn't without friends. He's a good spender and always ready to lend a helping hand to anybody who needs it. Folks at the mines and here in town like him. Slade Gumbert thinks highly of Rawlins, and going up against Slade Gumbert isn't my notion of something nice to do.'

25

'I'll agree with you on that,' Skelton replied. 'Where is Gumbert? I haven't seen him around the place here today.'

'I passed him over to the livery stable a little while ago,' Morton told him. 'He was just putting his horse away. Been down to the mines, he said. He's got an interest in one down there, you know. He'll probably be here most any minute now.'

'Gumbert owns the Deuces Up,' Skelton explained to Hatfield, 'and he's a cold proposition, though nice enough so long as he ain't crossed.'

Morton beckoned a waiter and ordered drinks. As they were consuming them, a man pushed through the swinging doors and crossed the room with slow, effortless strides, to the far end of the bar.

'That's Gumbert,' Skelton said in low tones to Hatfield.

Slade Gumbert was a tall man, loose-jointed, and slightly stooped. His face was lean almost to cadaverousness. He was blond as to hair and coloring, with pale blue eyes set deep in his head. His nose was long and straight and drooping at the tip above a wide, firm mouth. He wore a long black coat, now thickly powdered with dust. The swung-back skirts of the coat revealed heavy guns swinging low on his lanky thighs.

A bartender handed Gumbert a sheaf of papers. The saloon-keeper proceeded to look

26

them over in a slow, methodical fashion. He nodded, reached for a bottle and a glass in the same unhurried fashion, and poured himself a drink.

'Gumbert never seems to move fast, no matter what he's doin',' observed Skelton.

'Then you've never seen him pull a gun,' Morton commented with a slight smile.

'You never did, either,' Skelton retorted. 'Nobody ever did. A gun just happens in Slade Gumbert's hand. Fastest gun slinger in Texas, I reckon, if not in the whole southwest, and he never misses.'

'I can't say I ever saw a faster,' Morton admitted, 'but I've heard of a man, who, if he's what folks say about him, might give Gumbert a hustle.'

'Who?' Skelton demanded incredulously.

'A big fellow over in northwest Texas,' Morton replied. 'I never saw him, but I've heard tell of him. Goes by a sort of funny name—The Lone Wolf. One of Bill McDowell's Rangers, a lieutenant. And what folks who have seen him in action say about him sounds plumb loco.'

'Well, *he'd* be plumb loco, no matter who he is, if he went up against Gumbert,' Skelton grunted. 'But I reckon that ain't liable to happen. Gumbert is law abidin', so far as anybody ever heard.'

'That's right,' Morton agreed. 'He's never been anything else, so far as anybody knows, during the year he's been here.'

Hatfield's lips twitched slightly. He couldn't help but be amused at this manifestation of the prevailing suspicion entertained by the average cowman for this saloon-keeper and gambler. That Slade Gumbert was a gambler, or had once been one, Hatfield had no doubt. His dress and general appearance evidenced that. Skelton's next remark confirmed his conclusion.

'Gumbert is almost as handy with a deck of cards as he is with a gun,' the Forked S owner said. 'I watched him do some tricks the other night. He made them paste-boards do most everything but yelp out loud.'

Morton nodded. 'But he never sets in a game, you'll notice. He never seems to do much of anything like other folks. Sometimes I get a notion he's not human. About the only ordinary thing he ever does is whistle.'

'Whistle?'

'Almost always when he's doin' somethin',' Morton replied. 'Real soft and low, and does a good job of it. About the only one I ever heard who could make a whistle sound like music. But the things he whistles! Gives you the creeps to listen to 'em much.'

'That's right,' agreed Skelton. 'I've listened to him. Queer soundin' things that make you feel sort of crawly under you skin. They get you. Reminds me of Yaqui drums beatin' back in the hills on a moonlight night. I've heard

28

them, down in *mañana* land, and the tunes Gumbert whistles makes me think of 'em. Has the same sort of a beat to 'em that works on you in time. Not that they sound bad, but you get a notion they don't belong to civilized folks.'

Hatfield listened to Skelton's ruminations concerning Slade Gumbert's musical leanings with interest. He glanced toward the saloonkeeper, busy over his accounts, and saw that Gumbert's lips were pursed.

CHAPTER FOUR

SHOT FROM THE DARK

Jim Hatfield possessed exceptionally keen hearing, and while the others talked, he listened intently, his black brows drawing together. He favored Gumbert with a contemplative glance and abruptly his lips twitched slightly and a light of understanding glowed in his eyes.

Morton finished his drink and stood up.

'I'll be seein' you tomorrow, Skelton,' he said. 'Hope to see you again soon, too, Hatfield.'

He waved his hand to Slade Gumbert and left the room. Skelton gazed after him.

'Nice fellow, Pres,' he remarked. 'Knows the

cow business and been around quite a bit. Was in Arizona, and California, and East for a time. When his uncle, old Caswell Morton, died last year, Pres came into the Bar M. He and old Cas never got along any too well, but he was the only kin the old man had. Cas was sort of old-fashioned and didn't take well to new notions, like Pres had. Pres has done better with the spread than Cas ever did, though.'

Skelton pushed back his chair and got up.

'Well,' he said, 'I reckon I'll be headin' back for my place. I sent the boys along before I came in. Didn't want them to get mixed up with Rawlins and his bunch. Have they been in here?'

'Rawlins was,' Slade replied. 'He said he and his men were headed for home. That was a while before you came in.'

'Best place for him,' grunted Skelton, reaching for his hat.

Hatfield also stood up. 'I think I'll go to bed,' he said. 'Didn't get much sleep last night.'

'Where you stayin'?' Skelton asked.

'I've got a room over the stalls in the livery stable around the corner,' Hatfield told him.

'Good place,' said Skelton. 'Old Bart has clean beds and no bugs, which is more'n you can say for most places in this pueblo. Wait a minute and I'll walk with you. Want to see Gumbert before I leave.'

30

He walked to the end of the bar and engaged the saloonkeeper in conversation. Both spoke in low tones, and although they did not glance in his direction, Hatfield had a pretty good idea that he was the subject under discussion, but he gave no sign.

'All right,' Skelton said, as he came back, 'let's go.'

They left the saloon together. Skelton chuckled.

'I asked Slade what he thought of you, Hatfield. Bet you couldn't guess what he said—not that he said it a mean way, mind you. He said just two words, but that's a good deal for Slade Gumbert.'

'What were they?' Hatfield asked, with a smile.

Skelton chuckled again.

'Plumb poison!'

Hatfield laughed aloud, but did not comment.

With Skelton still chuckling over Gumbert's laconic observation, they walked up the street to the alley where the livery stable stood. They had reached the dark mouth of the lane when Hatfield half turned, then with a movement too swift for the eye to follow, hurled Skelton to the ground. At the same instant he went sideward and down himself.

A stream of fire gushed from the alley mouth. The buildings rocked to the roar of a gunshot. A slug whined angrily over Skelton's prostrate form. Another fanned Hatfield's face with its lethal breath. Then both of Hatfield's guns let go with a rattling crash. Hatfield rolled over, scuttled sideward and again the long Colts streamed fire.

And despite the storm of lead raking the alley from side to side, still a third shot boomed from the darkness there.

Hatfield felt the result of that one. It hit the ground right in front of him, stung his face, and filled his eyes with gravel and dust. With an oath, he slewed aside and fired blindly until the hammers of his guns clicked on empty cartridges.

Skelton had got some breath back into his lungs by now and also was shooting and bellowing curses.

'Hold it!' Hatfield shouted, blinking to clear his vision. 'We've either got him already or he's hightailed. Listen!'

Skelton ceased firing and they strained their ears. Hatfield thought he heard a patter of swift feet far down the alley, but because his head was still ringing from the roar of his own guns, he could not be sure. He stuffed fresh cartridges into the cylinders of his Colts.

'You stay here,' he told Skelton, and went zigzagging into the darkness of the narrow lane.

Nothing happened. He could see nothing in the blackness between the buildings, and when he paused an instant, the only thing he heard was Skelton pounding toward him, swearing lustily. That, and distant shouts from somebody who had heard the shooting.

'He's gone,' Hatfield said, 'if he isn't on the ground somewhere in here, and I don't think he is. Why didn't you stay back there as I told you?'

'Stay back there, huh!' Skelton bawled indignantly. 'Think I'm goin' to let somebody else do my fightin' for me. Let's see if we can find the sidewinder.'

They started forward again, cautiously, only to halt as a voice said from the darkness.

'That'll be far enough, gents!' An ominous double click emphasized the warning.

Hatfield's guns jutted forward, but Skelton had recognized the voice.

'Uncock that old baseburner, Bart!' he shouted. 'Do you want to blow a buildin' down? It's Raines Skelton. Fetch a lantern.'

There was a grumbling of oaths and the sound of shuffling feet. The old stablekeeper stumped from the open door, a lantern in one hand and a cocked six-gauge, double-barrelled shotgun in the other. The muzzles, that looked about the size of nail kegs, were jerking in all directions.

'Put them hammers down!' barked Skelton. 'If that thing lets go there won't be enough left of anybody for a buryin'. Put 'em down, I say!'

Old Bart obediently uncocked the huge weapon. Skelton ducked wildly as the barrels

33

lined directly with him during the process.

'He's cross-eyed, too,' he told Hatfield. 'You never know which way he's lookin'. Don't think he knows himself. Hand me that lantern, Bart, and keep them muzzles down.'

A careful search of the alley revealed no trace of the would-be drygulcher.

'But he'd have got me if it hadn't been for you, Hatfield,' Skelton declared. 'I won't forget it. Well, I'm headin' for home before some other Bradded R hand comes gunnin' for me. There's never goin' to be any peace till them sidewinders are run plumb off this range.'

Grumbling curses under his mustache. he headed back up the street to where his horse was hitched. Hatfield shook his head, and explained to old Bart what had happened.

Before going to bed, Hatfield cleaned and oiled his guns. As is often a habit with men who ride much alone, he talked to the big Colts as he would to his horse.

'Things are getting interesting in a hurry,' he murmured. 'Skelton figures that drygulchin' gent was after him, but he didn't stop to think that it was just chance that he, Skelton, walked to the alley mouth with me. He wouldn't have done it if he hadn't been talking about what Slade Gumbert had to say about me. Now certain folks know I aimed to hole up in old Bart's stable tonight and would be along this way sooner or later. It's beginning to look as if somebody is taking a little more than casual interest in me.

'Who? That's a question. I sort of riled a couple of outfits today, and maybe somebody in one bunch or the other was more riled than he let on to be. Must have been put considerable on the prod to try killing from the dark. And, so far as I could judge, none of those fellows looked to be just that sort. Can't tell, though. Some folks are good at hiding their real feelings.

'But it sure looks funny. Looks like somebody might know more about me than they're letting on. Which is liable to make things more interesting for me, if that happens to be so. Well, maybe we'll find out about that later.

'If not too late,' he added grimly, and went to bed.

Hatfield arose early the next morning. He ate breakfast at the Deuces Up, and then located the sheriff's office, which fronted the county jail. He found the sheriff at his desk, with the coroner beside him.

Cooper, the coroner, was a white-whiskered old frontier doctor with keen blue eyes. He started when Hatfield entered the room, but said nothing. The sheriff glanced up inquiringly, and greeted Hatfield with a wave of his hand.

'I was just thinking, suh,' Hatfield said, 'that seeing as I was the one who found him, I'd like

35

to ride up there with you when you go for Buster's body.'

'Don't reckon there's any objections to that, Hatfield,' said the sheriff. 'Meet Doc Cooper, our coroner. Doc's goin' along, too.'

Hatfield shook hands with Cooper. The sheriff closed a drawer of his desk and rose to his feet.

'We might as well be movin',' he said. 'I'll go hitch up. You fellows can get ready. I'll meet you here in front of the office.'

In short order the buckboard which Sheriff Dwyer drove up trundled out of Crater on its grisly errand. Doc Cooper sat on the seat beside the sheriff. Hatfield forked Goldy.

'I've dreamed about horses like that, but never expected to see one,' the sheriff remarked admiringly, running his eyes over the great sorrel.

'Old Goldy will do, I reckon,' Hatfield agreed.

'You don't often see a golden sorrel like that with a jet-black mane and tail,' the sheriff commented. 'Usually they're some off-colored. Nearly eighteen hands high, isn't he? Sure got a look of speed, too. Doc, he even tops Pres Morton's roan, and I didn't think there was a finer horse than that roan in all Texas.'

In a little less than an hour the buckboard swerved around the bend north of the spot where Hatfield had discovered Clem Buster's hanged corpse. Sheriff Dwyer leaned forward, peering ahead. Abruptly he barked an oath and jerked his horses to a rearing halt. Hatfield pulled up sharply. The three men sat staring toward the great tree branch extending across the shadowy trail. Sheriff Dwyer finally broke the silence.

'I—I'll be damned!' he stuttered. 'There—there's two of 'em!'

Dwyer was right. Beside Clem Buster's corpse, another body swung at the end of a noosed rope.

Sheriff Dwyer sent his horses charging forward. He pulled up again beneath the tree and stared.

'It—it's Bob Hawley of the Forked S!' he gulped.

Again the three men stared wordlessly at the body swinging gently in the breeze. Hawley had been a fair-haired young fellow of medium size. Between his bulging eyes was a small blue hole.

Doc Cooper scrambled to the ground and moved closer. 'Killed by a gunshot wound, and his body noosed up quite a while later,' was his verdict.

'The same as Buster,' Hatfield commented.

Doc Cooper shook his white head. 'Dwyer,' he said to the sheriff, 'there'll be the devil to pay over this. Raines Skelton will swear the Bradded R bunch did it to even up for Clem Buster. And who can blame him! Now you have got a cattle war on your hands!'

The sheriff swore explosively, including both the Forked S and the Bradded R in his vituperations. He shook his fist angrily. Then abruptly he cooled.

'I'll hitch the horses and we'll cut down the bodies,' he said.

Jim Hatfield had been staring intently toward the swinging bodies. As Dwyer strode off to find a convenient trunk for hitching, Hatfield moved closer to the coroner.

'Doc,' he said in low tones, 'take charge of those two ropes. Don't let them out of your hands. I'll tell you why later.'

'All right,' Cooper agreed. 'If you say to do it, there must be a good reason.'

'There is,' Hatfield said.

Having tied the team, the sheriff returned. Hatfield swarmed up the tree trunk, hitched his way out onto the overhanging branch and loosened the knots that secured the ropes to the limb. He gently lowered the bodies to the ground. Dwyer and Cooper carried them to the buckboard and deposited them in the bed of the vehicle. Hatfield walked about under the tree and eyed the ground intently.

'Doc,' he asked as the coroner joined him again, 'didn't it rain a little last night, right after dark?'

'That's right,' Cooper replied. 'Not much, but it was sort of brisk for a few minutes. Why?'

'Right under the tree here, where the leaves

are thin, are two different sets of boot tracks,' Hatfield pointed out. 'You'll notice they are both pitted by big rain drops. Don't forget that, Doc. It might be mighty important, later on. It rained right after dark, and I'm sure it didn't rain any more during the night. The stars were shining brightly when I went to bed, late. And there were no signs of later rain this morning.' He repeated earnestly: 'Don't forget, Doc.'

The old doctor shook his head. 'Those eyes of yours don't miss anything,' he said. 'I won't forget, Jim. I've got the ropes, too.'

CHAPTER FIVE

MARSHAL OF CRATER

As the grim procession rolled up to the coroner's office, silent men lined the main street of Crater. But when a second body was sighted, and identified, the crowd broke up into talking, gesticulating groups. It was a near riot! Sheriff Dwyer curbed the excitement then after the bodies were disposed of, he hurried back to his office to confer with his deputies. Hatfield lingered in the coroner's office after the sheriff had gone. Doc Cooper shut and locked the door and sat down with Hatfield at his desk, upon which lay the two lengths of rope.

'McDowell send you over here, Jim?' Cooper asked.

'That's right.' Hatfield nodded. 'He got your letter and decided I'd better give the situation a once-over. Looks like you got the making of a first class cattle war here, Doc.'

'We have,' Cooper declared grimly. 'When Raines Skelton hears of this, there won't be any holdin' him. And Rawlins is just as bad. He'll be ready for all the trouble Skelton can bring him, and before it's finished, the whole range will be mixed up in it. Another "to the last man" ruckus in the makin' all right, if it isn't stopped in a hurry. What about those ropes, Jim?'

'Doc,' Hatfield told him slowly, 'those two ropes are from the same piece. I'd say both came originally from a twenty-five foot hair reata used for tethering or picketing. Whoever used it to hang Buster and Hawley cut it in two.'

'You're sure both pieces came from the same twine, Jim?'

'Absolutely,' Hatfield said positively. 'This is an unusual braid, Doc. See how the black and white hairs intertwine to form a peculiar pattern? Even if the cut ends didn't match, as they do, it would be mighty strange if two of these things showed up in the same vicinity. I saw a couple of them once. Over at the State Prison. An inmate of the prison braided them and sold them to visitors. They were exhibited in the front office. He couldn't have made many of them, because it's a long and tedious process, fashioning a rope patterned like this one. I sure wish I had had a look at that prisoner while I was at the warden's office, but of course I had no reason to, at the time.

'Maybe he's there yet?' Doc remarked hopefully.

Hatfield shook his head. 'No. Not unless he's back on another charge, which I don't think is the case. The warden told me something about him when he showed me the ropes. I didn't pay much attention to what he said at the time, but I do remember that he said the fellow had served a couple of years and was about due to be released, with time off for good behavior. Wouldn't have been discussed at all if it hadn't been for the ropes. They encourage the inmates to put in their spare time making useful things, and the warden was proud of that fellow's work. So you see, it's mighty unlikely that two of the things should show up here this way at the same time. Anyhow, the cut ends match perfectly to continue the pattern. You can take it from me that Buster and Hawley or their dead bodies, rather, were hanged with the same rope, presumably by the same person.'

Doc Cooper gave a low whistle. 'And what does that mean?' he asked.

'I'd sure like the answer to that one,'

Hatfield said grimly.

'What about those boot marks you mentioned?' Cooper asked.

'Those boot marks were undoubtedly made by the men who hanged the bodies,' Hatfield declared. 'There were two sets—one under Buster, the other under Hawley. And both sets were made before the rain. It was less than an hour till dark when I run onto Buster's body. The rain fell right after dark. Which means that Hawley's body was hung then, between the time I rode north with Rawlins and his bunch and when the rain fell, only a short time after we reached town.'

Doc Cooper looked bewildered.

'Don't you see it, Doc?' Hatfield asked. 'Skelton proved conclusively that he couldn't have had anything to do with Buster's killing. Rawlins proves just as conclusively that he couldn't have had anything to do with the killing of Hawley. Rawlins didn't know anything about Buster's killing and the hanging of his body until he saw the body there on the trail. He rides to town with me, he and his bunch. And while they are riding to town, somebody sneaks Hawley's body to that tree and hangs it beside Buster's.'

'Maybe done by some other members of the Rawlins outfit,' hazarded Cooper. 'He didn't have all his hands with him last night.'

'I thought of that,' Hatfield replied, 'although it's highly unlikely. But, if they did,

42

how come they had half of the rope with which Buster's body was hanged.'

Doc Cooper threw out his hands. 'I give up,' he said. 'It is your business to find out about things like this, and you've certainly got your work cut out for you this time.'

'I'm inclined to agree with you,' Hatfield admitted ruefully.

'Yes, it looks like Rawlins and his bunch are in the clear where Hawley's killin' is concerned,' Cooper went on, 'but try and get Raines Skelton to believe that! Jim, there's perdition in the makin'!'

After the coroner's inquest, with the jury bringing in a verdict that declared the deceased met their deaths at the hands of parties unknown, the town of Crater remained as tense as a hair-trigger. Discussions raged in the saloons, with occasional violent arguments. Men stood about the streets in low-talking groups. But Sheriff Dwyer and his deputies patrolled constantly and the day and the night following passed without serious incident. Nothing had been heard from either the Forked S or the Bradded R.

'They know now what's happened, though,' men said. 'This ain't finished.'

Jim Hatfield went to bed late and slept rather longer than usual. He was eating his breakfast in the Deuces Up when a wild-eyed man rushed in. Hatfield recognized him, because the man had been pointed out to him the day before, as Quent Maltby, the mayor of the town of Crater.

Maltby glanced around the room, and rushed up to Slade Gumbert, who was standing in his customary position at the far end of the bar.

'Slade,' he exclaimed excitedly, 'Bert Rawlins and the Bradded R bunch are in town! They're holed up in the Last Chance Saloon at the east end of Main Street, and they're loaded for bear! Raines Skelton and his Forked S boys are headed for town to shoot it out with Rawlins! They'll be here any minute.'

Gumbert remained his usual imperturbable self. 'Well, what you botherin' me about it for?' he asked. 'Go tell the sheriff and have him throw 'em all in the calaboose.'

'The sheriff ain't here!' Maltby sputtered. 'He left town two hours back with his deputies after Pres Morton sent word there'd been a wideloopin' over to the Bar M and that he and his hands had the sidewinders holed up in White Horse Canyon. He sent to Dwyer for help in roundin' 'em up. John headed for the Bar M in a hurry. So I come to you.'

'What in blazes do you want me to do about it?' demanded Gumbert. 'I'm no sheriff.'

'No, but you're the only man I know of who can do anythin',' urged the mayor. 'We haven't had a town marshal since Sydenstricker resigned last week. I've got the power to appoint somebody to fill the vacancy. I'm appointing *you* marshal of Crater!'

'Like thunder you are!' growled Gumbert. 'I ain't mixin' in this ruckus or or takin' sides. I'm in business here and don't aim to get tangled with my customers. Guess again, Maltby.'

The mayor swore in helpless fury. 'What in blazes am I goin' to do?' he demanded. 'There'll be shootin's and killin's here in the next twenty minutes if somethin' ain't done. Who can I get to act? I ain't no gun fighter!'

Slade Gumbert turned slowly and gestured toward the table where Jim Hatfield was just finishing his breakfast

'There's the man you want,' he said quietly. 'Appoint him town marshal, and there won't be no ruckus.'

Maltby stared at Hatfield. 'The feller who found Clem Buster's body and kept Raines Skelton from gettin' his head blowed of the same night?' he muttered. 'I don't even know him, Gumbert.'

'You don't need to,' Gumbert replied. 'All you need to do is get him to take over the chore.'

'Cuss it to blazes, I'll try anything!' the mayor swore in desperation. He strode to Hatfield's table. 'What do you say, feller?' he asked. 'You heard. Will you take over the marshal's job? Pays two hundred a month.'

Hatfield finished his coffee with deliberation. He gazed at the excited mayor,

45

his green eyes thoughtful, the concentration furrow deepening between his black brows. He set down his empty cup and rose to his feet.

'Yes,' he said. 'I'll take it, for today, anyhow.'

Mayor Maltby's face brightened as his eyes ran over Hatfield.

'You sure size up big enough, anyhow,' he declared. 'Here's the badge, got it right in my pocket. Pin it on your shirt. Anything else you want?'

'One thing,' Hatfield replied. 'But I'll take care of that. Skelton will come into town from the west, won't he?'

'That's right,' answered the mayor. 'Chances are they'll hitch their horses at the big rack over there by the corral and come ahead on foot. You'll hear 'em comin'. There are a lot of young fellows in Skelton's outfit, and they'll be kicking up plenty of racket.'

Hatfield nodded. 'I'm going over to the livery stable a minute,' he said. 'Be right back.'

'You'll do better on your feet!' the mayor expostulated.

'I'm not going for my horse,' Hatfield said, and passed through the swinging doors.

'What in blazes does he want from the livery stable?' the mayor complained wonderingly.

'I don't know,' said Gumbert, 'but I'm willing to bet that whatever it is will be bad hearin' for Skelton and his bunch.'

The mayor was willing enough to agree with

46

Gumbert's prophecy when Hatfield returned a few minutes later, for across his arm he carried old Bart's six-gauge shotgun. He opened the breech and shoved two plump cartridges in the huge bores.

'About the only way a man can go up against a bunch of twenty-five or thirty packing sixes and hope for anythink like an easy break,' he commented, 'is with a scattergun. I've noticed that even a salty outfit don't like the taste of buckshot at close range any too well.'

'That thing ought to be mounted on wheels,' grunted Gumbert, eyeing the six-gauge askance.

Even as he spoke, in the distance sounded a stutter of shots.

'Here they come!' yelped Mayor Maltby.

A smile twitched Hatfield's lips. 'You men stay here,' he said, and sauntered out the door.

The shooting was swiftly drawing nearer. Hatfield could now hear whoops and yells, and swiftly then the patter of fast hoofs, though still quite a way off. They slowed abruptly, then ceased altogether. The shooting also stopped.

'They're unforking now,' Hatfield told himself. He walked up the street to the alley upon which the livery stable fronted. Stepping into the narrow space between the flanking buildings, he waited.

The shooting and yelling were resumed, closer now and steadily drawing nearer.

'Let 'em blaze away,' Hatfield muttered. 'By the time they get here, most of 'em will have empty guns in their hands, and it takes a minute or two to reload.'

Louder and louder sounded the uproar. Then Hatfield could hear boots thudding in the dust. He waited a moment longer, stepped from the alley then, and faced the approaching Forked S cowboys. He swung the six-gauge around to cover the group.

'Halt!' he shouted. 'Drop those guns and put up your hands!'

The group jostled to a standstill, staring in amazement. A scant half dozen yards away, the black shotgun muzzles yawned toward them, and behind those rock-steady muzzles stood Hatfield.

'Hatfield!' bawled Raines Skelton, who marched in the van. 'What in the eternal are you hornin' in on this for?'

The shotgun muzzles moved the merest trifle, to cover Skelton point-blank.

'I'll down you, Skelton, if one of your men makes a move!' Hatfield warned. 'You'll never know what hit you. Get your hands up!'

The shotgun hammers clicked back to full cock.

That was enough for Skelton. His hands shot skyward. 'Get 'em up boys,' he ordered. 'That son of the devil means it!'

Thirty pairs of hands jerked into the air. Those holding guns let them thud on the

48

ground.

Hatfield stepped a little to one side, the shotgun still trained on Raines Skelton.

'All right,' he called. 'Get going, right up the street single file. And don't take any chances. This thing packs fourteen buckshot to the barrel, and it'll spray you like a hose. Move!'

They moved, cursing and muttering, hands pointing stiffly upward.

'Where you takin' us?' demanded Skelton.

'I'm taking you to jail,' Hatfield told him. 'Keep going!'

CHAPTER SIX

PLUMB POISON

Shambling along, the men in the line were glaring, but they made no threatening move. The black muzzles followed them like ominous twin shadows. Hatfield fell in behind, and still a little to one side, alert and watchful.

As the seething cowboys scuffed their high heels through the dust in front of the Deuces Up, a derisive yell sounded from the open door.

'Ho-ho-ho!' bellowed Slade Gumbert. 'Paint this one on your chuck wagons! Skelton, didn't I tell you he was poison?'

'Come along, Gumbert,' Hatfield called. 'I

49

want you. You, too, Mayor Maltby.'

'Sure,' Gumbert chuckled as he fell in alongside the marching line. It did not make the Forked S bunch feel any better to note that Gumbert's black coat skirts were swung back, and that his thumbs were hooked over his double cartridge belts.

In front of the sheriff's office, Hatfield halted the line.

'Face the wall,' he ordered. 'Gumbert, disarm those men.'

Gumbert strode forward. 'I'm sort of hauled into this it seems, gents,' he told his victims cheerfully, 'so please don't do nothin' to make me nervous.'

He plucked guns from holsters and tossed them across the street. Skelton was the last to be relieved of his hardware. He growled and muttered, but offered no resistance.

'Open the door, Maltby,' Hatfield directed the mayor. 'Go in and unlock the bull pen.'

The mayor hurried into the office. Keys jingled. There was a creaking of hinges.

'All right!' he called.

'Inside, gents,' Hatfield ordered. 'Keep right on moving.'

Hatfield herded the last cursing cowboy through the office and slammed the iron door after him. The bullpen was packed to suffocation.

'We can't breathe in here!' howled Skelton.

'You should have thought of that before you

50

started this row,' Hatfield called back to him. 'Think about it till I get back.' He turned toward the outer door.

A big, hard-faced cowhand shook his fist through the bars.

'Fellow, if you wasn't wearin' that marshal's badge!' he threatened.

Hatfield let his level gaze rest on the cowboy's anger-convulsed face for a moment.

'Wait,' he told him, and headed for the door.

'Where you goin'?' asked Mayor Maltby.

'To the Last Chance,' Hatfield called over his shoulder. 'Understand there's another bunch down there that needs taking care of.'

'Good gosh!' gulped the mayor. 'Is he goin' to tackle that Bradded R gang, too?'

'Reckon he'll tackle anything,' chuckled Gumbert. 'Come on, Quent, let's go watch the fun down there.'

Hatfield walked steadily down the street until he was opposite the Last Chance. The place was ominously quiet. He started across the street.

'That's far enough, Hatfield,' a voice warned through the window. 'Come any closer and we'll drop you!'

'And stretch rope, the lot of you,' Hatfield instantly countered, tapping the badge on his breast. 'You're bucking the Law, Rawlins, and you're not big enough to do that.'

With the same unhurried stride he crossed

the street. Nothing happened. He shoved through the swinging doors and glanced around the room.

The Bradded R punchers stood in a compact group, hands on their guns.

Hatfield surveyed them coldly over the barrels of his shotgun.

'All right,' he told them. 'Clear out of here, fork your broncs and get out of town, pronto!'

'You think we're goin' to let Raines Skelton say he ran us out of town?' shouted Bert Rawlins.

'Want to see Skelton?' Hatfield asked.

'You're cussed right I want to see him!' shouted Rawlins.

'Then ride past the calaboose, and you'll see him peekin' through the bars,' Hatfield said. 'Now, get going. You've got ten seconds to clear this room. Anybody here when time's up will go into jail with the Forked S bunch, and it's almighty crowded in there already. Move!'

Bert Rawlins stared at Hatfield, his jaw sagging. He clamped it tight, shook his red head.

'Come on, boys,' he said quietly. 'We're headin' for home.'

As the Bradded R punchers jostled through the swinging doors, the raucous laughter of Slade Gumbert boomed outside.

Hatfield watched the Bradded R outfit fog it out of town. Then he walked back to the sheriff's office with Gumbert and Maltby.

They found the bullpen seething with discomfort and profanity.

'You can't do this, Maltby!' fumed Raines Skelton. 'When I get out of here—'

'Who said you were goin' to get out?' challenged the mayor.

Skelton fairly danced with rage. Hatfield's eyes crinkled slightly at the corners.

'Ready to hold court, Your Honor?' he asked the mayor, with great gravity.

Mayor Maltby sat down importantly behind the sheriff's desk. He cleared his throat, glowered at the suddenly silent prisoners.

'Raines Skelton,' he said, 'for bustin' up the peace, I'm sentencin' you fellers to thirty days in the calaboose!'

A wail of woe went up from the bullpen.

'With sentence suspended durin' good behavior,' concluded the mayor, with a wide grin. 'Marshal, open the door.'

Hatfield obediently swung back the iron door. The prisoners crowded out. Raines Skelton glared at Hatfield, then suddenly leaned against the sheriff's desk and roared with laughter.

'Never been made such a fool of since the last time I bucked my mother-in-law!' he declared, wiping his streaming eyes. 'But darn it, I like it! Come on boys, let's go home. It ain't safe around here.'

'Just a minute,' Hatfield said. He unpinned the badge and laid it on the desk. 'I'm resigning,' he told Maltby.

His eyes singled out the cowboy who had threatened him through the bars.

'Fellow,' he said softly, with easy-to-understand meaning, 'I'm not wearing a marshal's badge now, and your hardware is lying right across the street.'

The big puncher shuffled his feet, fumbled his hands, and dropped his gaze.

Then he looked up defiantly.

'Think I aim to get locked up again for bustin' the peace?' he demanded in injured tones. A grin split his hard face. 'If it's just the same to you, I'd like it a heap better if you and me shook hands.'

They did.

Mayor Maltby watched the Forked S outfit head west, and breathed a sigh of relief.

'But it ain't finished,' he declared pessimistically. 'Them fellers ain't changed their minds one bit. Hatfield cooled 'em down for right now, but they feel just the same about things as they did when they rode into town. They'll get together sooner or later, see if they don't. A couple of weeks and the big fall roundup starts, and that means they'll be all around the range and bound to meet up with each other. Anyhow, maybe they will keep it out of town. Hatfield, why in blazes did you have to go and throw up the marshal's job? With you wearin' that badge I wouldn't have anythin' to worry about.'

'A marshal is sort of restricted to town and doesn't pack any authority outside,' Hatfield explained.

'You're right, there,' agreed the mayor. 'I'm goin' to have a talk with Sheriff Dwyer as soon as he gets back to town.'

Slade Gumbert turned to the door. 'I'll be gettin' back to my place,' he announced. 'Business will be boomin' today. And just wait till they hear about it over at the mines!'

He left the office. Hatfield picked up old Bart's shotgun.

'I might as well take this back to the stable,' he said. 'Don't figure I'll need it any more today.'

'No, thank Providence!' said Mayor Maltby, fervently.

Silent groups watched Hatfield's progress along the street. Behind him, talk swirled and eddied, with much wagging of heads.

After disposing of the shotgun, Hatfield repaired to the Deuces Up. A noisy crowd was in the place, drinking and talking.

There was a momentary silence at his entry, but the conversation was soon resumed as the drinkers emptied and refilled their glasses.

Slade Gumbert stood at the far end of the bar, alone. His pale eyes were brooding. He nodded as Hatfield walked over to him. There was nobody within easy hearing distance.

'Gumbert,' Hatfield said in low tones, 'how long since you left the river boats?'

The saloon keeper started. He stared at his questioner.

'How in blazes did you know I was on the Mississippi boats?' he demanded.

'Guess work,' Hatfield replied. 'I've been over there, and seen quite a few of the steamboat dealers. Had trouble over there, didn't you, Gumbert?'

Slade Gumbert stiffened. His eyes took on a glassy look.

His long, flexible hands dropped to his sides, the fingers spread.

'Man,' he said, a trifle thickly, 'folks don't ask personal questions like that in this country.' His fingers spread a little wider as he spoke.

Hatfield made no move. Only his eyes seemed subtly to change color a little.

'Not unless they expect a straight answer,' he instantly countered. 'Don't try it, Gumbert. I'm sure you know better.'

'Yes,' Gumbert admitted quietly, 'I know better. I'm good, but I wouldn't have a chance ...' All right, I'll come clean. I'm wanted in Louisiana, for a killin'.' His eyes met Hatfield's steadily.

Hatfield nodded.

'I'm not particularly interested in things that happen in another state,' he said slowly, 'and there are killings *and* killings.'

'It was one of those things that happen on the boats,' Gumbert said. 'Five aces in a deck.

56

I'll tell you all about it.'

He began talking, and as he spoke, Jim Hatfield visioned the scene on the steamboat tied to the wharf of a small town. He saw a tall, icy-eyed man standing behind a gambling table, a blazing gun in one hand, a torn ace of spades in the other. On the table lay a second ace of spades.

Across the table, a stricken man reeled and fell.

'That was the way of it,' concluded Gumbert. 'But they don't look at such things over there like they do here, and a river gambler wouldn't have much chance in those small town courts. So I cut and run for it. Swam the river and got away. Swore off cards that night. Haven't sat in a game since, and that was three years back. I drifted west. Had a little money and bought this place. Been doin' right well with it, too. I play square with my customers, and I run straight games.'

Hatfield nodded again. 'Keep on running them straight, Gumbert,' he said. 'It'll pay in the end. And I've a right smart idea you are going to keep on doing well here for a long, long time.'

A smile suddenly brightened his stern face. He turned and left the room.

Slade Gumbert watched his tall form pass through the swinging doors, and on his face was the look of a man from whose shoulders a heavy burden has suddenly been lifted.

'Goin' to keep on doin' well for a long, long time,' he repeated. 'From him, that's as good as another man's oath. I reckon I haven't got anything to worry about any more.'

CHAPTER SEVEN

HIRED HAND

Well after dark, Sheriff Dwyer got back to town. Hatfield, Gumbert and Mayor Maltby were eating together at a corner table in the Deuces Up when, dusty and disgusted, he entered.

'They got away,' he announced sourly as he slumped into a chair and called for a drink. 'We had 'em penned in that box canyon, all right, but they set fire to the brush in there and slid over the rimrock under cover of the smoke. When the fire burned out and things cooled off enough for us to go in, there wasn't a sign of 'em. They must have had almighty good horses. I wouldn't have believed a mountain goat could have gone up those slopes.'

'Get a look at any of them?' Hatfield asked.

'Nope,' grunted the sheriff. 'Morton didn't either, though he was pushin' 'em close when they slid into the canyon. He told me they were wearin' masks. They holed up behind the

rocks in there and held him and his men off.'

'How about the cows they rustled?' asked Maltby.

'They didn't take them in the canyon with 'em,' said the sheriff. 'Reckon they're scattered all over Morton's south range. He'll have to comb 'em out of the brakes again. He was gettin' ready for the roundup and now he's got all the work to do over. He's sort of mad about it.'

'Anybody get hurt?'

Dwyer shook his head. 'Morton got a hole in his hat, but that's about all. Considerable shootin', I take it, but no damage done t anybody. Morton rode to town with m Stopped off at the general store. He'll be h after a while, I reckon.'

The sheriff had already heard of the happenings in town.

'You did a prime chore, Hatfiel complimented the Lone Wolf. 'A plum job. A whole troop of Texas Rangers have done it better.'

Slade Gumbert's thin lips twitche There was an amused look in his pale

The others had drifted away an was alone at the table when Pres M in, some time later. Morton gla nodded, and came over to the tab

'I guess I'll have somethin' t 'Want to talk to you, anyhow, H about today, but I'm told you

the marshal's job permanent.'

'It's not exactly in my line,' Hatfield replied. 'I just gave Maltby a hand.'

Morton nodded. 'Reckon you're like most cowhands,' he commented. 'You feel more at home on a horse.'

'That's about the size of it,' Hatfield agreed.

'I was talking with Skelton about you,' Morton went on. 'Raines would like to sign you up with his outfit, but he tells me you don't want to be takin' sides in the row hereabouts.'

'Right.' Hatfield nodded.

'Well,' said Morton, 'I'm not takin' sides, either, as everybody knows. I can use a few more tophands, specially with the roundup comin' on. How about it?'

Hatfield considered a moment, his eyes thoughtful. 'I reckon I could do worse,' he finally agreed to the implied offer of a job. 'It looks like you hired yourself a hand.'

Jim Hatfield rode to the Bar M with Morton he following morning. He was riding toward eath, and he knew it.

Hatfield found the Bar M good range, but rd to work. Lying east of Rawlins' Bradded it curved around it to the south to sprawl miles between the Terlingua Mountains to east and the Mist River Hills to the west. great Forked S, extending far to the north roughly shaped like an L, embraced the ded R in its half square.

The east and west pastures of the Bar M's south range were slashed and pitted with canyons and draws, where cows holed up to escape the heat. Most of the gorges were grass-grown and watered. Beefs grew fat and sleek and exceedingly frisky within their shadowy recesses. Combing them out was a considerable task.

The Bar M riders however were tophands, though for the most part, they were a taciturn and uncommunicative lot of cowboys. They accepted Hatfield without comment, and quickly learned to respect his ability.

Recognizing and appreciating Hatfield's unusual talents, Morton assigned him to the difficult and rather hazardous southwest pasture. Working with him was another new hand, a fresh-faced, blue-eyed youngster, Billy Wagner, recently down from the north.

'I'm glad Morton put me on with you,' Wagner confided to Hatfield as they rode out. 'I like to have somebody to talk to, and about all you can get out of most of this bunch is grunts. Besides, they're most of 'em Arizona or New Mexico men. They handle a rope and a horse sort of different from Texas riders. Latigos instead of trunk straps on the saddles, and center fire hulls!'

Hatfield permitted himself a smile. Wagner was typically Texan, and held no brief for methods not peculiar to the Lone Star State.

He was a likable youngster, however, and

knew range work. Hatfield liked him from the start.

'Sort of lonesome in the bunkhouse, too, for a young feller,' Wagner went on to unburden himself. 'Nobody there but them old daddies who worked for Morton's uncle before he died. The new men, the boys from Arizona, sleep in the ranchhouse.'

Hatfield nodded, his eyes thoughtful over that remark, and changed the subject.

Hatfield and Wagner worked in the shadow of the grim Mist River Hills. Their jagged crests of naked rock towered darkly into the blue of the sky, and their boulder-strewn slopes, sparsely grown with scraggly vegetation, gleamed coldly in the sunshine and frowned ominously when the dark of evening came.

Those bleak hills interested Hatfield. They had an inscrutable look, as if they veiled an ancient mystery. And their rugged slopes appeared practically unclimbable.

Back among those desolate and broken crags, Hatfield knew, was the grim gorge known as Mist River Canyon.

'Nobody ever been in there and lived to tell about it, I reckon,' Pres Morton had told him. 'I doubt if you could even see into the canyon from the rimrock, even if it was possible to get there. It's a good eight miles from one end to the other, and I reckon the water runs in there like a mill race. Nothin' but drownin' for anything that gets swept in there, if you ask me.'

Hatfield was inclined to agree with Morton, and thought of the cows he had seen hurtled into the dark mouth of the gorge.

When Hatfield encountered Raines Skelton in town a couple of days later, the rancher was thinking of that, too.

'Lost another big herd,' he told the Ranger. 'Trailed 'em to the bank of Mist River, just north of the canyon. I'd sure like to line sights with the sidewinder who did it. It's bad enough to have your critters widelooped and run off, but to have 'em drowned like so many kittens sure makes a man paw sod.'

The following morning, leaving Billy Wagner searching the nooks and crevices of a brush-grown canyon, Hatfield rode south along the base of the Mist River Hills. As he progressed south, the vegetation thinned, the grass grew scant, until he was riding over a sandy desert dotted with chimney rocks and buttes and occasional patches of greasewood or sage. Grotesquely shaped cactuses put in an appearance, and the heat noticeably increased.

More and more rugged grew the hills, their color changing to raw reds and yellows, luridly reflecting the sun's rays. The desert became more austere as it rolled southward toward the distant Rio Grande.

Finally Hatfield sighted a thread of green that he knew must be the struggling growth bordering Mist River after it flowed from its canyon, ultimately to dissipate its waters in the thirsty sands.

The southern rampart of the hills was a towering battlement of reddish stone that thrust up sheer from the desert's floor.

Hatfield turned Goldy and rode beneath the cliffs. Three miles, and he rounded a bulge and sighted the mouth of Mist River Canyon, less than a hundred yards distant. He pulled rein on the river bank and sat gazing down at the water, flowing from the mouth of the gorge.

He instantly noticed several things. First, the south mouth of the canyon was much wider than its northern entrance. Also, the river here was wider and shallower and more sluggish than where it entered the gorge ten miles to the north.

His black brows drew together as he scrutinized the stream. Finally, he drew a note-book and the stub of a pencil from his pocket and began writing figures on a blank sheet, pausing from time to time to estimate the width of the stream and the apparent depth of the water. He closed the note-book and gazed at the canyon mouth.

'Goldy,' he said, 'here's a funny one. Unless my calculations are way off, and I don't think they are, there's a lot less water comes out of that canyon than flows into it up north. Now what's the answer to that one? May not mean anything much, but it may mean a lot. I sure would like to get a look into that crack farther north.'

He pondered the notion of sending the sorrel upstream through the shallow appearing water, but decided against it. Goldy's legs were too precious to risk on such a venture, unless the need was urgent. Hatfield raised his eyes to the sun-shimmering cliff tops. He shook his head doubtfully, turned Goldy and rode back the way he had come.

Several more days followed without event, days of hard work and regular ranch routine. Hatfield began to wonder if he hadn't made a mistake, and was riding an off trail.

'It sure looks that way,' he decided. 'Nothing seems to be happening down here. The only thing worth noticing is the fact that Wagner and I are kept alone on the southwest range, and that doesn't mean much. New hands on a spread usually get the more unpleasant assignments. That's only natural and holds good for any business.'

And then things began to happen.

Mid-morning found Hatfield working a narrow canyon thickly grown with tall brush. The canyon was a box with perpendicular sides and end wall. Down its center ran a considerable stream of water.

Hatfield was forking a rangy bay, an excellent rope horse, equipped with a worn but serviceable stock saddle, of which Morton had several hanging in his barn. Hatfield seldom used Goldy for ranch work on rough ground, not caring to expose the sorrel to the danger of injury.

That watered, grass and brush-grown canyon was ideal for a hole-up for cattle, but to his surprise, Hatfield combed the gorge to its head without flushing a single cow.

'Looks almost like somebody had worked over this crack recently,' he mused as he turned the bay down canyon.

In deference to long habit, while doing his work in a quiet, efficient manner, Hatfield continually took stock of his surroundings. Every thicket or clump or chimney rock came in for careful scrutiny as he rode. He noted the movements of birds on the wing or of little animals in the brush.

He was nearing the canyon mouth when abruptly his gaze fixed on a thicket a couple of hundred yards ahead. Over the thicket a bluejay was tumbling and darting with angry cries.

'That little fellow's actin' up funny,' he muttered. 'Something's sure got him on the prod. Snake on a limb, maybe, or a wild-cat in the brush.'

Nevertheless, he gave the thicket careful attention as he approached it.

The sun was almost overhead, its vertical rays striking downward through the growth.

Suddenly Hatfield slewed sideward in his saddle. He left the hull in a streaking dive. The bay, startled by the unexpected move, reared high.

There was the thud of a bullet striking flesh, the crack of a rifle. From the thicket swirled a streamer of blue smoke.

The bay screamed once, crashed over on its side, twitched a moment and was still.

CHAPTER EIGHT

A LOST TRICK

Hatfield was behind the carcass of his horse before the bay's limbs ceased jerking. He slid his rifle from the boot which, fortunately, was on the upper side of the dead horse. Another bullet thudded into the body. A third screamed over it.

Hatfield thrust the rifle barrel across the body and raked the thicket with a stream of lead. A fourth shot answered the volley.

'Want to play tag, eh?' he muttered to the hidden drygulcher. 'Well, we're liable to have some fun before you smoke me out.'

The next moment, however, he realized that that was just what the drygulcher had in mind—to smoke him out, literally.

A blue streamer swirled up from the thicket, rapidly thickened. A sprightly crackling sounded from the depths of the growth.

'Set fire to the brush!' Hatfield exclaimed, staring at the thickening column. 'And he's back behind it waiting for me! If I try to get through on either side, he'll drop me like a settin' quail!'

The brush was dry and the fire spread with astonishing rapidity. In a matter of minutes, a sheet of fire extended from wall to wall of the narrow canyon, and, driven by a favorable wind, was racing up the gorge.

Having no more fear of bullets for the moment, Hatfield scrambled to his feet and headed upcanyon at a swinging trot. Soon, however, he was forced to quicken his pace. The fire was rolling after him like a galloping horse.

'Outsmarted!' he thought disgustedly as he lengthened his stride. 'They've got plenty of wrinkles on their horns. They let things ride along quiet and peaceful for a week without making a move, but they've been keeping tabs on me all the time. Figured out that I was keeping Wagner within easy distance at first, and waited till I got careless and let him drift off on his own. Just as soon as he was well out of the way and no chance of him spotting what they aimed to do, they twirl their loop!' He raced on, panting. 'I'm liable to pay heavy for the mistake. Unless I get a break, or something, it's mighty apt to be my finish. This brush grows thick right to the head of the canyon, and nothing but a lizard could go up those walls! If I can't find a crack or cave to slide into, I'm going to be the prime attraction of a barbecue!'

As he loped up the gorge, he eyed the side walls in hope of discovering some crevice into which he might slip, but the dark cliffs towered unbroken. The smoke was getting thick, the heat between the encroaching walls increasing. The canyon drew the fire into its depths with a mighty draft, the end wall being somewhat lower than the sides.

Hatfield was breathing heavily long before he realized he had reached the head of the gorge. The fire was close at his heels, and whirling brands and soaring sparks momentarily threatened to start a blaze ahead, that would cut him off between two sheets of flame.

He sighted the end wall, where the stream began in a great spring that bubbled up from the ground. Had it run from under the canyon wall, he might have sought sanctuary there.

Grimly he counted his chances. The sum was not encouraging. The fire was but a few hundred yards behind him. Its crackling and roaring filled the gorge with a pandemonium of ominous sound. Sparks stung his flesh and smoldered in his clothes. Burning brands darted at him. The smoke clouds swirled around him in a suffocating mist. The air rushing up the gorge was like the blast from the mouth of a furnace.

At last, though, he reached the head of the canyon. Before him towered the pitiless, unclimbable end wall. Behind was the advancing wall of flame. He glanced around, shook his head. There appeared no possible avenue of escape.

'One chance,' he muttered, 'and that one not so good. Have to try it, though. Nothing else to do.'

He ejected the shell from his rifle barrel and left the breech open. Then he slid into the still, fairly deep waters just below the bubbling spring. Holding his head above surface, he rooted a couple of small boulders from their beds. Easing back in the water, he rolled these upon his chest. As an afterthought, he whipped his neckerchief loose and bound it tightly over his nostrils. Then he placed the muzzle of the rifle in his mouth, clamping his lips closely about it, and eased his head under water until it rested on the muddy bottom a good eighteen inches below the surface.

The lock of the rifle, with the breech open, extended above water level. He could breathe, after a fashion, the air that filtered down through the barrel.

'Now if I don't get boiled, I may be able to hold out,' he told himself. 'The brush is thinnest up here next to the end wall, and once the fire gets here, it should burn itself out in a hurry. Just a matter of hanging on, but that's liable to be difficult.'

It was. Breathing through the gun barrel was no easy task. To make matters worse, the smoke laden air invoked an urge to cough, and coughing with an iron tube in the mouth and a strip of cloth bound tightly across the nose was a somewhat complicated matter, and, under the circumstances, pretty sure to guarantee death by strangulation.

The air became almost too hot to breathe. Hatfield could feel the water of the stream becoming warm. Belatedly he realized that he had neglected to remove the cartridges from the magazine of the rifle. If the iron, above water, got hot enough, they would explode, and then it would be his finish for sure.

The fire was all around him now. The veil of water over his eyes, when he cautiously opened them to stare upward, was a marvel of exquisite coloring, scarlet and amber and violet and rose, as the flames flickered over the surface and the smoke clouds rolled. Awful as was his position, Hatfield could not but appreciate its awesome beauty.

But it was more important that he think about more than the beauty of flame kaleidoscoped by moving water. More smoke than air was coming down the rifle barrel. His lungs were laboring, and the water pressure on his body did not help. He began to experience a queer distortion of time and distance. It seemed as if he had lain on the muddy bottom for an eternity with untold eons stretching before him.

The flame curtain of the water receded to a tremendous distance, then rushed close again, only to recede once more. In his ears was a tolling as of all the church bells in the world, and behind the metallic clanging was a roar like the rending apart of creations. Hatfield knew he was on the verge of unconsciousness, and to lose his senses would inevitably mean death.

With a mighty effort of will be got a grip of himself. Fighting madly against the encroaching world of fantasy that threatened to engulf him he forced himself to think of ordinary, everyday things—his horse, his beginnings as a Texas Ranger, his college days before that. Anything to give the real ascendancy over the unreal.

And then, with a surge of hope, he saw that the flame curtain clothing the water had dimmed to a uniform gray. That could mean but one thing. The fire had burned itself out for want of fresh fuel. Now only the smolders and the thinning smoke clouds held sway beyond his watery sanctuary.

Cautiously he raised his head until it was above water, blinking as the stinging smoke seared his eyes.

The canyon was still blanketed with a fogging mist. But the air was breathable, and the up-draught was swiftly thinning the smoke pall. Already the sun was showing through.

Another moment and its rays were pouring down hotly from a cloudless sky.

Hatfield crawled out of the water. He felt stiff and sore all over. There was a ringing in his ears and a queer shaky feeling to his limbs. Undoubtedly he had been near his end.

With trembling fingers, he drew his guns and made sure that they were in perfect working order. He did not worry about the effect the wetting would have on his well-greased ammunition; and the strong and simple mechanism of the heavy Colts would not suffer.

He drew out his sodden tobacco and papers and spread both on a hot rock to dry, which they did quickly. He emptied boots and wrung most of the water from his clothes. Then, feeling chilly, a strange contrast to his recent sensations, he managed to roll a cigarette and stretched out in the sun to warm and dry. A few drags of fragrant tobacco smoke and his nerves quieted. He gazed at the sky with puckered eyes and conned over the situation.

'Well, they took this trick, all right,' he told himself. 'And come mighty close to taking the game. But they tipped their hand at last. Now I know definitely they are on to me and out to do me in. They won't catch me asleep again.'

He rested for nearly an hour, then got to his feet, rather stiffly, and headed down the canyon. Flickers and smolders still dotted the floor of the gorge, but the wind had dissipated the smoke. And the light, quick-burning brush had not too greatly heated the rocks.

Before he had gone far, Hatfield heard a shot, down-canyon, then another and another, evenly spaced.

'Billy Wagner coming looking for me,' he deduced.

He drew his gun and fired an answering shot to allay the young cowboy's fears.

Soon he saw Wagner fogging his way up the gorge through the powdery ash.

'Tarnation and blazes, fellow!' shouted Wagner. 'I was afraid you were a goner. I remembered you sayin' you were goin' to work this hole today, and when I saw the smoke boilin' up and realized it came from the canyon, I sure got a bad feelin'. What set it?'

'A match, I reckon,' Hatfield said drily.

Wagner shook his head. 'Could be,' he admitted, 'but how anybody as careful as you are with matches and tobacco could start a brush fire is past me. I've a notion some careless cowhand was traipsin' around down here. Did you see anybody?'

'Nope,' Hatfield replied, with truth.

'Got your horse, eh?' continued Wagner.

'He died from a bullet,' Hatfield answered.

Wagner clucked sympathetically. 'Reckon there was nothin' else for you to do,' he said, drawing the conclusion Hatfield wished him to, for the moment, anyhow. 'But what I'd like to know is how in thunder you managed to keep from getting cooked.'

Hatfield told him. The young cowboy shook his head in admiration.

'Plumb smart,' he applauded. 'Me, I'd never have thought of that. I won't forget it. Might come in handy some time. Uh-huh, plumb smart. Well, climb up behind me. I think this critter will pack double.'

Wagner's dun groaned a little under Hatfield's two hundred pounds, but offered no serious objection to the added burden.

Both he and his riders were glad when they cleared the smoky, dusty canyon and were out on the range once more.

Hatfield let Wagner do most of the talking when they reached the ranchhouse, merely corroborating the cowboy's story of how he, Hatfield, had been trapped in the canyon by fire.

'Brush fires around here at this time of the year are bad,' said Pres Morton, shaking his head. 'You were mighty lucky, Hatfield. Lucky, too, there wasn't a bunch of cows holed up in there.'

'Yes,' Hatfield agreed, 'it was—lucky.'

Morton insisted that Hatfield take a day off to rest up after his harrowing experience. So, late the following afternoon, Hatfield rode to town. He entered the Deuces Up and found Slade Gumbert at the end of the bar, as usual.

Gumbert was regarding, with little favor, a group of five men drinking together farther up the 'mahogany.'

'Where do they all come from?' he demanded queruously of Hatfield. 'This town seems to be the stoppin' off place for all the owlhoots and slick iron artists in Texas. If that bunch is up to any good, I sure miss my guess. Look at the way their guns are slung. And you can't hear a thing they say, two steps off.'

'Tied-down holsters,' Hatfield commented. 'Well, I never knew a gent who tied down the ends to live long. They're plain advertisement that he's either looking for or expecting trouble.'

'That bunch is lookin' for anything that isn't nailed down,' grumbled Gumbert. 'I'm sure keepin' an eye on my strongbox tonight.'

The men in question did have the look of being tough hombres. They wore the garb of the rangeland, which showed signs of much hard riding, but so far as Hatfield was able to see, their hands bore no marks of rope or branding iron, although doubtless all had been cowhands at one time or another.

But despite Gumbert's pessimism, the quintet created no disturbance. They drank quietly for some time, conversing together in low tones, sat down at a table and consumed a hearty meal, had another drink or two, and then left in a body.

Hatfield also left the saloon a little later, slipping out unobtrusively and walking along the street in a leisurely fashion until he

76

reached the rack where Goldy was tied. When he had hitched the sorrel there, earlier in the evening, he had noted the five horses bearing certain meaningless Mexican brands that were already tethered to the pins.

Before he reached the hitchrack, the horses in question passed him, heading east. Forking them were the men who had attracted Gumbert's unfavorable attention. They glanced neither to right nor left and apparently took no notice of the Lone Wolf.

Hatfield did not quicken his pace, but when he reached the rack, he untied and mounted Goldy with speed. He then sent the sorrel east along Main Street at a slow walk.

CHAPTER NINE

TRUMPING A TRICK

It was a blue and silver night, with a sky spangled with stars and a thin slice of moon in the west. As Hatfield cleared the outskirts of the town, he saw the five horsemen some distance ahead of him. Pulling Goldy up, he waited until they were shadowy blurs on the trail. Then he sent the sorrel forward again.

Jim Hatfield relied on his own unusually keen eyesight to make the trailing of the five possible. He felt that he should be able to keep the group in sight and at the same time remain unnoticeable himself, riding as he did at the edge of the trail and taking advantage of shadows cast by the frequent clumps of growth.

'May be just a useless ride, but somehow or other I've got a hunch about those men,' he mused. 'They left town like gents definitely headed for somewhere, and with things to do.'

The riders continued steadily east for several miles. Then they turned off at a fork that veered more to the south. The track, Hatfield knew, was the road to the Terlingua Mines to the southeast of town and beyond the Bradded R's east pasture.

Suddenly Hatfield's interest quickened. Just beyond the forks, a man had ridden from the shadow and joined the group.

For nearly two hours after that the group rode steadily east by south. Far behind, a moving shadow amid the shadows, drifted Goldy and Hatfield. Finally, in the last light of the dying moon, Hatfield saw a dark cluster of buildings ahead, close to the rearing bulk of the Terlingluas. One structure much larger than the others stood out against the mountainside.

The group turned from the main trail and rode toward the settlement which Hatfield knew must be the mining town of Terlingua. He spoke to Goldy and the sorrel increased his pace. The horsemen ahead had disappeared

78

from sight in the shadow of the tall, dark building at the base of the mountain.

Terlingua was a shack town populated by the large number of workers who found employment in the nearby mines. Once each month, on pay-day, the miners descended in a body on Crater for a pay-day 'bust' and on those days Crater was lively indeed.

Tomorrow was pay-day and everybody had gone to bed early to rest up in anticipation of the morrow's celebration.

The town was dominated by the huge, gaunt structure, set on a little plateau above the rude dwellings that housed the stamp mill. Tonight the windows were dark save for one golden square that marked the office.

In the office, the paymaster and two clerks were busy making out the pay-roll and filling the envelopes that would be passed out to the miners early the next morning. As a routine matter of precaution, a guard sat in the office with a shotgun across his knees, a rifle ready to hand. The Terlingua Mines had never had any trouble and didn't expect any, but what was considered adequate provision was taken against the possibility.

The office was warm and comfortable. The monotonous hum of voices calling and checking figures was soothing. The guard, the heels of his boots hooked over a rung of his tilted-back chair, drowsed halfway between waking and sleeping.

He was wide awake enough, however, when the outer door suddenly banged open. Wide awake, but not soon enough. Before he could more than clutch at his shotgun, he found himself looking into the black muzzle of a long-barreled .45. Behind the six-gun was a masked face with only glinting eyes showing. And behind the masked gun holder were five more masked men, their guns trained on the paymaster and the clerks.

The guard opened and closed his mouth like a stranded fish, no words coming forth. The man with the gun was doing all the talking.

'On your feet,' he ordered, his voice harsh and muffled behind the black folds of his mask. 'Let that scattergun fall to the floor . . .' Now turn around and face the wall, with your hands up and against it. Stay there, and nothing will happen to you. Move, and you get it . . .' All right, boys, herd them pencil pushers over alongside him and get busy.'

'Is—is this a robbery?' stammered the paymaster.

'Naw,' replied the gunman, 'it's just a game of checkers, and it's your move!'

The paymaster moved as the forward jutting Golt emphasized the command. The next instant he was facing the wall, his trembling hands pressed against it. His clerks were ranged alongside him.

One of the robbers strode to the table and began stuffing the envelopes and loose money into a sack. The leader, a broad-shouldered man of little above medium height, searched the room with a swift glance that centered on the big iron safe over to one side. The door was closed, apparently locked.

'Open that box over there,' he ordered the paymaster, giving him a dig in the ribs with his gun muzzle.

'I—I can't,' the paymaster squawked. 'I don't know the combination. Nobody but the treasurer knows it, and he isn't here.'

'Sure you're not lyin'?' growled the owlhoot. 'Maybe a little fire on your back will make you remember the combination.'

'Honest, I don't know it!' quavered the paymaster, his limbs shaking.

The bandit regarded him a moment through his mask holes, nodded his head.

'Guess you don't,' he agreed. 'If you did, you wouldn't be that scared. Don't matter, anyhow. Here, Brade, keep your gun on these hombres.'

One of the robbers left the table and stood guard behind the prisoners. The masked leader strode to the safe and squatted beside it, his ear pressed against the steel door, his slim, steely-looking fingers deftly twirling the combination knob.

For a minute or more he twirled the knob forward and back with the utmost nicety. Suddenly there was a soft clicking sound. The bandit grunted with satisfaction and swung the door open. He began tossing thick packets of bills to the man with the sack.

'Foldin' money,' he remarked. 'Thought there ought to be some around. They pay bills with it in town. The metal is for the rock busters who like to hear their dinero jingle.'

Swiftly the safe was emptied. The man with the sack jerked the pucker string tight. The leader arose from the safe and strode across the room with a last quick, all-embracing glance. At his nod, one of his men picked up rifle and shotgun. Another relieved the guard of his belt gun.

'All right,' said the leader, 'let's go.'

He whirled as a voice rang through the room:

'Not just yet! Elevate!'

In the doorway stood Hatfield, a gun in each hand.

The broad-shouldered leader was behind his men. With the speed of light he went sideward and down. His gun boomed even as Hatfield went along the wall, firing with both hands. Lances of flame spurted through the darkness, bullets thudded against the wall. The place was a pandemonium of yells, screams, curses, the boom of guns and the crash of smashing furniture.

With a clang-jangle of breaking glass and splintering woodwork, the window went to pieces. Boots thudded on the ground outside. Hatfield fired at the sound, whirled and bounded for the open door. His knees hit the squalling paymaster, who was scuttling around on all fours.

He sailed through the air and hit the floor with a crash that shook the building.

Half-stunned by the force of the fall, it took Hatfield some little time to flounder to his feet and get his bearings. He rushed outside, stuffing fresh cartridges into his empty guns.

Lights were flashing up in the shacks. The shouts of the aroused miners added to the tumult, though which Hatfield's keen ears caught the sound of horses' irons beating swiftly into the distance.

The moon had set and the night was now black. Pursuit was out of the question.

Half-clad men were running toward the office, volleying questions.

'Inside!' Hatfield shouted to one bearing a lighted lantern.

The office was a shambles of broken glass and smashed and overturned furniture. Three bodies lay on the floor. A dead hand still grasped the stuffed money sack.

'Three of 'em got away, including the leader who opened the safe,' Hatfield growled.

Holding the lantern high, he glanced around the room at the damage that had been done. The guard's scalp had been nicked by a bullet and he looked sick but, Hatfield decided, he had suffered no serious damage. One clerk had a hole through the fleshy upper part of his arm. The gibbering paymaster and the other clerk were untouched.

As more lanterns arrived, Hatfield strode over to the wounded clerk, who was little more than a boy. He was sitting in a chair beside the overturned desk, gripping his bullet-punctured arm to lessen the bleeding, and swearing softly behind his clenched teeth.

'Good man! You can take it!' Hatfield spoke approvingly as he cut away the sleeve to bare the injured member.

'I'm not a fightin' man, but if I ever line a gun on those double blasted lobos, I'll—' the clerk swore.

'Hope you get the chance,' Hatfield said. 'And I'm thinking if you do, you won't miss.'

Hatfield quickly fashioned a tourniquet and controlled the bleeding. Then he hurried out to his horse, quickly returning with a roll of bandages and a small pot of antiseptic ointment which he always carried in his saddle pouch. He deftly bandaged the wound and fashioned a sling to support the young man's arm.

'That'll hold you till we get you to Crater,' he told the clerk. 'Doc Cooper can take care of it right, then.'

'I don't believe he'll do any better job than you have,' grunted the clerk, taking a long drag at the cigarette Hatfield rolled and lighted for him. He added significantly: 'But he won't be able to do much for those gents on the floor

84

you took care of.'

The demoralized paymaster had recovered enough to ask questions.

'I saw them turning off toward the mill,' Hatfield told him briefly, 'and figured they were up to no good. Thought I'd better have a look-see.'

The paymaster turned to the miners who now were crowding the office.

'Boys,' he said, 'here's the man who saved your pay-day for you. And saved the company a good many thousands more, as well.' He nodded toward the open safe.

The building shook to spontaneous cheering. The grinning hard-rock men patted Hatfield on the back, crowded around to shake his hand.

'Shure and the b'ys would have been mortal disap'inted to have their cilibration put off,' declared a giant red-headed foreman who was almost as tall as Hatfield and even broader. 'We hope to be seein' ye in Crater tomorrow, sor. Shure and ye won't be lackin' for a wee drap of the crature whin we meet.'

Hatfield nodded his appreciation of the invitation, but made a mental resolve to steer clear of the big foreman and his 'crature' that was soon to be released from the prisoning bottle. He turned his attention to the guard's creased scalp.

CHAPTER TEN

THE LONE WOLF

Once the wounded men were cared for, Hatfield squatted beside the dead owlhoots and removed their masks. He instantly recognized them as three of the five men he had seen drinking in the Deuces Up.

'But the one who started things—the big he-wolf of the pack—got away all right,' he muttered. 'I'm willing to bet a hatful of pesos he was the rider who joined the other five below the trail forks.' He raised his glance to the open safe. 'Did they make you open it, or was it open already,' he asked the paymaster.

'Neither,' the man replied. 'One of them, the one who seemed to be giving the orders, worked the combination and opened it.'

Hatfield stared at the man. 'Sort of unusual for this country,' he remarked.

'He did it in less than a minute,' the paymaster went on. 'I don't know the combination, but I do happen to know it is an intricate one. It didn't seem to bother him, though. If he had know it, he couldn't have worked it more quickly or easier.'

Hatfield gazed at the safe, his eyes thoughtful. 'How about the pay-roll money?' he asked suddenly. 'You wouldn't have left that lying here in the office.'

'There is a small safe in the main mill office,' replied the paymaster. 'It would have been put in there after we finished making up the pay-roll. This safe here contains the private papers and documents of the mine owners as well as usually a considerable amount of cash.'

'Who knows the combination?' Hatfield asked.

'The company treasurer is the only person here regularly who knows it,' the paymaster replied. 'Of course the president knows it, and perhaps some other high officials. I can't say as to that. Perhaps, too, some of the larger stockholders may know it. I'm not sure about that, either.'

'Know who those stockholders are?' Hatfield asked.

The man mentioned several names, all unfamiliar to Hatfield. Then he added:'Raines Skelton also holds considerable, and Slade Gumbert, who owns a saloon in Crater, has a big block. Gumbert got in on the ground floor when the company was first formed and production wasn't much to brag about. He's about as big a single stockholder as we've got. But the treasurer is the only one around here now I can say for sure knows the combination.'

Hatfield nodded, the concentration furrow deepening between his brows.

'Where's the treasurer?' he asked suddenly.

'Went to Crater this afternoon. Not expected back until tomorrow.'

Suddenly the man's eyes dilated. 'You don't think—' he began thickly.

'No, I hardly think they got hold of him and forced him to divulge the combination,' Hatfield replied, 'although it is possible. My guess is that either somebody acquainted with the combination let it slip, by accident or design, or that the robber leader is an experienced safe cracker, something not often met with in west Texas. The boys out here use dynamite or sledge-hammers.'

'That's right,' agreed the paymaster. 'I never heard of anything like this before—not in this country.'

'You always make up the pay-roll at night, the night before pay-day?' Hatfield asked.

'We always have,' the paymaster replied. 'After the mill shuts down, as it always does for pay-day, and things are quiet.' Then he declared emphatically: 'But they won't do it again, if I have anything to say about it. And if they do, you can wager I won't be here to handle it. I lost five years off my life tonight.'

'An inch more to the right with that cussed slug and I'd have lost all I got comin' to me off mine,' growled the guard. 'That's the first time I was ever caught settin', and gents, it's the last!'

Hatfield grinned. He felt that the guard meant it. 'Let's see what these owlhoots have

88

in their pockets,' he suggested. 'Might find something that ties them up with somebody.'

However, the miscellany of odds and ends turned out of the pockets proved to be of no significance. Hatfield was about to give up the search when his probing hand encountered a folded slip of paper. He deftly palmed it and slipped it into his own pocket without the others noting the action.

The search completed, Hatfield stood up, and spoke to the paymaster.

'Have this wounded boy taken to Crater in a buckboard or wagon,' he directed. 'And notify Sheriff Dwyer of what happened. 'I'm heading back to the Bar M. Got to work tomorrow.'

The paymaster accepted without question the order of the tall cowhand who appeared to have usurped all the authority in sight. And he thanked Hatfield profusely for his timely assistance.

When Jim Hatfield was some distance from the mining town, he took the folded paper from his pocket, struck a match and examined it by the flickering light. His brows drew together over the seemingly meaningless jumble of figures scrawled on the town sheet:
6076, 6077, 6081, 6084, 6074—Crater—Thursday
6051

'What in blazes?' he wondered as the match flickered out. 'Crater, that's plain enough. Thursday, that's today—yesterday, rather, since it's past twelve midnight—but what about those numerals? The bottom one has all the appearance of being intended for a signature. Since when have owlhoots started going by numbers? This is a puzzler.'

Hatfield slipped into the Bar M bunkhouse so quietly he did not awaken the slumbering punchers. With scarce two hours of sleep, morning found him showing no results of his hectic night.

He rode south with Billy Wagner and went to work on the west range again, combing out beefs, sawing a few horns and branding a few calves.

The day passed without event. Hatfield was still puzzling over the cryptic figures written on the sheet of paper, and still unable to make head or tail of them.

When he and Billy Wagner got back to the ranch-house, shortly before dark, they found a visitor waiting. It was Sheriff John Dwyer. The sheriff greeted Hatfield warmly.

'Son,' he said, 'you sure have raised Hades and shoved a big chunk under a corner since you lit on this range. That was a fine job you did down to the Terlingua, almost as good as the one you did durin' the twenty minutes you were town marshal of Crater. We hauled them three sidewinders back to town today. They haven't showed any signs of gettin' up and walkin' away. Doc aims to hold an inquest on 'em tomorrow, just to keep in practice, I reckon, and he wants you there.

'I spoke to Morton, and he said all right. He ain't feelin' so good himself, Pres ain't. His horse fell with him last night when he was ridin' back from town. Pitched him in a brush patch and skinned his face up some and wrenched his leg. He's limpin' bad. Said he aims to put in a day or so in bed.'

'Sorry to hear about it,' Hatfield replied. 'All right, I'll be with you tomorrow.'

'Why not ride back to town with me tonight?' suggested the sheriff. 'We'll be company for each other and I've got a spare bed in my place.'

Hatfield agreed, and after eating, he and the sheriff set out together.

'Them three holdups you downed were hard-lookin' hombres,' said the sheriff as they jogged along. 'Everybody took a look at 'em, and Slade Gumbert spotted 'em right off as three of a bunch of five that was in his place early yesterday evenin'. Slade said he sure didn't like their looks then and recalled mentionin' it to you.'

Hatfield nodded.

'That's right,' he agreed.

Sheriff Dwyer turned in his saddle and bent a searching glance on Hatfield.

'Say,' he said, 'did you happen to be ridin' down toward Terlingua last night plumb by accident?'

Hatfield shook his head. 'No,' he admitted.

'I didn't like the looks of those fellows, either, so when they rode out of town, I trailed them.'

'So I thought,' the sheriff said. 'Trailed 'em to the stamp mill, and tackled all six of 'em! By the way, where did the sixth one come from? There was only five in the Deuces Up?'

'That's something I'd mighty well like to know. He joined them just below where the trail forks.'

The sheriff shook his head and swore, then he faced Hatfield again, gazing long and earnestly at his stern profile etched in pale flame by the moonlight.

'Hatfield,' he said, 'just who are you, anyhow?'

'I told you my name, and it's my real one,' Hatfield replied, with a ghost of a smile.

'Uh-huh, Jim Hatfield of—' The sheriff waited expectantly. Hatfield's smile held. '—the Texas Rangers,' he finished.

'I knew it!' the sheriff declared. 'Couldn't be anything else.' He uttered an explosive exclamation. 'And I've got you spotted, sure as shootin'! You're the Lone Wolf!'

'Been called that,' Hatfield admitted.

'I should have known that, too, right off,' said the sheriff. 'Nobody else could do the things you've done since you landed here. Nobody else since the days of Wyatt Earp could have done what you did in Crater when you stood off the Forked S and the Bradded R. Wyatt used to do things like that, when he was marshal of Dodge and Ellsworth and Wichita, but nobody else ever did till you came along. Raines Skelton told me that when you lined him with that six-gauge, he felt wings sproutin' on his shoulders!'

'It was largely bluff on my part,' Hatfield said, and smiled. 'I wouldn't have had much chance if they had cut loose on me.'

'Uh-huh,' the sheriff remarked drily. 'Uh-huh, bluff, but a bluff none of thirty salty cowhands cared to call. Any more than Bert Rawlins and his bunch cared to call the one you run on 'em in the Last Chance. You can call it bluff, but I reckon those boys saw it as four aces pat.'

Hatfield laughed and changed the subject.

'Hear anything more from Skelton or Rawlins?' he asked.

'I sure have,' the sheriff told him disgustedly. 'Rawlins came stormin' in yesterday mornin' to tell me he'd lost more cows drowned in Mist River canyon. Swore his losses were cripplin' him and if they kept up much longer he'd lose his spread. He declared that's just what Skelton and the others want to happen, and I couldn't talk him into seein' it any other way. He left swearin' he'd shoot any Forked S rider he caught on his range, on sight, and you know the Forked S hands often take a short cut across the Bradded R to get to their southwest range.'

Hatfield looked grave.

'With the big roundup starting next week, I'm afraid we're in for trouble,' he said. 'Those two outfits are bound to meet then. It's going to be a chore to keep something bad from happening.'

'I've thought of that,' the sheriff admitted, 'and right this minute I'm thinkin' of a little plan that may help a lot. You'll find out about it when the time comes.'

'I'm not quite ready to let out that I'm a Ranger,' Hatfield said. 'I'm not sure the men responsible for all this ruckus raising know I'm one. They may, but I rather believe they think I'm just another owlhoot aimin' to horn in on their game. I'd like to keep under cover a little while longer, if I can.'

'What I'm thinkin' about is liable to help you do that,' said the sheriff.

When they reached Crater, Dwyer suggested they drop in and see the coroner before going to bed. Hatfield, still pondering the cryptic notations on the slip of paper in his pocket, absently agreed.

Doc Cooper was up and pottering around when they entered his little office. The first thing that caught Hatfield's eye was the two sections of hair rope with which the bodies of the slain cowboys, Clem Buster and Bob Hawley, had been hanged. Doc had them festooned on pegs back of his desk.

Hatfield gazed at the grisly things and his mind returned to the visit he had paid the state prison warden several years before, when he had seen ropes of a similar pattern displayed in a case in the office devoted to the souvenirs manufactured by the prisoners.

Suddenly his eyes glowed. He uttered an exclamation under his breath.

'Sheriff,' he said aloud, 'Doc knows I'm a Ranger, has known me for years, so we can talk freely in here. There's something I want you to do for me. I want you to send a telegram to the warden of the State Prison. I'll tell you what to say. Get a pencil or pen and write it down. I want the answer to come to you. Hold it for me.'

Sheriff Dwyer started in bewilderment at the message Hatfield had dictated. He read:

Do the numbers: 6076, 6077, 6081, 6084, 6074, and 6051 mean anything to you? Especially relative to the inmate who braided souvenir hair ropes of a peculiar pattern and was released from prison about two years ago.

'What in blazes does it mean?' asked the sheriff.

'I took this slip of paper from the body of one of those owlhoots in the stamp mill at Terlingua,' Hatfield explained, handing the slip to the sheriff. 'It sure had me puzzled for a while, then all of a sudden, when I looked at that rope back of Doc's desk, a rope I am certain was braided in the State Prison, it came to me that perhaps those numbers were the serial numbers of former prison inmates.'

'Yes?' prodded the sheriff.

'Yes, and I believe they are a sort of code, used by the head of the outfit responsible for the trouble going on here, for the purpose of calling the bunch together when he means to pull something like the robbery attempt at Terlingua. If the hunch is a straight one, it may give us a line on him. It is often possible to trace the movements of a former prison inmate and identify him even if he is operating in another vicinity and under another name. See?'

'Uh-huh, I see,' replied the sheriff.

'Maybe I'm following a wrong hunch,' Hatfield smiled. 'We'll know after we get the warden's reply.'

'The nearest telegraph office is at Foster, twenty-five miles to the north of here,' said the sheriff. 'I'll start for Foster as soon as it gets light in the morning, and I'll wait there for the answer.'

'And,' said Hatfield, 'if the hunch turns out to be a straight one, send a wire, in my name, to Captain McDowell at Ranger Post headquarters, asking him to try and trace the movements of those men since they were released from prison. Perhaps you can arrange to have McDowell's answer relayed to you here.'

'I'll take a deputy with me, and hole him up in Foster till the answer comes,' said the sheriff. 'This thing is beginnin' to look promisin'.'

'Maybe,' Hatfield conceded. 'If we can just get past the roundup without a conflagration bustin' loose.'

CHAPTER ELEVEN

A BOSS IS CHOSEN

Coroner Cooper's inquest on the following morning, held that Hatfield had been justified in killing the three robbers, and commended him for the act, adding a typical cow country rider to the verdict to the effect that it was a 'blue-blazing' shame he didn't manage to down the other three varmints while he was at it.

Shortly after dark, Sheriff Dwyer got back to Crater with the State Prison warden's answer to Hatfield's query.

6076, JOSEPH BOWERS; 6077, WILLIAM BOWERS; 6081, PHILIP HORN; 6084, JOHN GREY; 6074, CHARLES HATCH; 6051, PETER MORROW. THESE MEN, WITH THE EXCEPTION OF MORROW, SERVED SENTENCES FOR CATTLE STEALING. MORROW WAS SENT TO PRISON FOR BANK ROBBERY. OPENED THE SAFE OF A BANK IN LAREDO AND ESCAPED WITH A LARGE SUM, BUT WAS LATER CAPTURED BY THE RANGERS. THESE MEN WERE RELEASED

'I fired the message to Captain McDowell, pronto,' said the sheriff. 'Tom McCarty is waitin' in Foster for Captain Bill's answer. He'll bring it to me the minute he grabs it.'

Hatfield nodded with satisfaction. 'Now we may get somewhere,' he said.

'Sure hope so,' said the sheriff. 'Let's go over to the Deuces Up and eat. Come along, Doc, you're always hungry.'

Slade Gumbert was in the back room when they arrived in the Deuces Up. He opened the door in answer to the sheriff's knock.

'Come in,' he said, holding the door wide. 'Just finishing up checking the day's receipts. Wait till I put the pesos away and I'll eat with you.'

He crossed to a small iron safe in the corner and squatted before it. Hatfield watched his slender, supple fingers manipulate the combination knob with the utmost nicety. The tumblers clicked, the safe door swung open. Gumbert placed the money inside and closed the door. He gave the combination knob a few deft twirls and straightened up.

'All right,' he said, 'let's eat.'

Gumbert ordered drinks and an excellent meal.

'Everything on the house tonight,' he

98

declared. 'I can afford it. Hatfield saved me considerable *dinero* down at Terlingua the other night. There was a lot of money in that pay-roll and in the safe. The stockholders would have had to stand the loss, of course.' He smiled as he saw them attack the food. 'Put it away, gents, plenty more in the kitchen when this runs out.'

During the days immediately following, Jim Hatfield experienced an unpleasant premonition that the mysterious developments of the Mist River country were fast building up to a climax.

Pres Morton had kept to his room for two days. When he finally did appear, he limped badly and his face was seared by the raw scabs of three deep cuts.

Young Billy Wagner met the owner as Morton left the ranchhouse on a tour of inspection, and expressed his sympathy.

'You sure must have had a bad spill, Boss,' he said. 'You look like you'd shoved your way through a glass window.'

Morton's reaction to this well-meant remark astonished and disconcerted the young cowboy. The rancher's scarred face flushed darkly red, his thin lips tightened until they were like a razor cut. His eyes glittered.

'You'd do better to keep your fool notions to yourself,' he spat at the young fellow and walked off with a stiff back.

'What in blazes was the matter with him?'

Wagner wondered as he later told his experience to Jim Hatfield. 'Darned if I didn't think for a minute he was goin' to pull on me. He actually took hold of his gun handle. He was as riled as a steer with a burr under its tail. Why should he go on the prod like that? I didn't do more'n ask him how he was feelin'.'

The answer to that one interested Hatfield, decidedly, although he did not hazard an explanation for Wagner's benefit. Instead, he deftly changed the subject, preferring not to have Wagner do too much speculating out loud over Morton's peculiar behavior.

Hatfield was conning over this and other recent events as he rode through the gold and scarlet glory of the autumnal rangeland. All about him was the beautiful peace of the dying year. The emerald of the prairie was tipped with amethyst that overlay the green like a veil of changing shadow. The deeper hollows were bronzed by the fading ferns, while the hill tops blazed crimson and cardinal and smoldering saffron.

The thin, fine line of the horizon had lost its sharpness and was mystically blurred by a cerulean haze. There was a hush in the air that not even the whispering of the keen-edged wind could dissipate. It was as if Nature were holding her breath in anticipation of what was to come.

And Hatfield had a feeling that the whole neighborhood was also holding its breath. An air of tenseness and apprehension prevailed whenever men got together, in town or on the range. There was an unwonted reserve in conversation, as if each man chose his words with care and forethought, fearful as to how the lightest remark might be construed. There was an increasing tendency to form into groups that avoided close contact with other groups. The babble of talk in saloons would abruptly still when a stranger or a not too well-known acquaintance walked past.

'They're taking sides, beginning to line up,' Hatfield told himself. 'And that's just what is to be expected.'

Hatfield knew that if real trouble developed, it would not concern only the Forked S and the Bradded R. The Mist River country was like any part of the West. Grudges and resentments existed between old inhabitants as well as between old and new. There were scores to be evened, wrongs, real or fancied, to be avenged.

Raines Skelton, the wealthiest and most influential rancher in the vicinity had undoubtedly trodden on some toes in his time. Those with sore bunions would remember. Others might well vision possible advantages for themselves through a lessening of Raines Skelton's importance.

And among the younger element, Hatfield was sure there were those who felt that Bert Rawlins was not getting altogether a square deal. For after all, there was no real proof that Rawlins had committed any off-trail acts. The chief indictment against him was that he was a recent settler on the range, the purchaser, operator and reviver of a spread an old-timer had let run down to near worthlessness.

'It's a nice kettle of fish, all right,' Hatfield told himself morosely, 'and how to get the fish out before they boil or spoil is more than I've been able to figure out as yet. But if we can just get past this darn roundup without blowing the lid off, I may have a chance to twirl my twine.'

Employing all his plainsman's skill to make sure he was not trailed, Hatfield took another ride south to the desert country. He followed the course of Mist River, south of the canyon, until the dwindling stream finally lost itself in the thirsty sands. He returned from this expedition deep in thought, but wearing a pleased expression.

'I believe I'm riding a straight hunch,' he told himself as he headed for the ranchhouse. 'Not a drowned cow down there anywhere. Of course, they could go down some fork of the river back there in the canyon, but I don't think so. It's hardly reasonable to believe that, admitting the possibility of the river branching in the canyon, all the carcasses would go one way. Well, it's up to me to find out for sure about that, but not until after the roundup. No time, or opportunity, now.'

Hatfield did not know it, but others were also impatiently waiting for the roundup to be over. In Pres Morton's room, several of his Arizona riders were gathered with their boss. A heated discussion was raging.

'We'll lay low till this cow collectin' is over,' Morton declared with finality. 'Things are too stirred up right now to suit me. And that big hombre over at the bunkhouse is plenty suspicious, and I believe Wagner is workin' with him. Otherwise, why did Wagner make that smart crack about me goin' through a window. I suppose Wagner, being young and uppity, couldn't resist takin' a dig at me when he saw my face all cut up.'

'Who in blazes is that big fellow, anyhow?' growled one of the hands.

'I've figured him out as being one of two things,' Morton said. 'Either he's some smart and salty owlhoot planning to run his own bunch in here and collect some pickin's for himself, or he's a Cattlemen's Association rider. One's as bad as the other, the way we're fixed. He knows darn well somethin' is goin' on, but I reckon he hasn't caught on to how it is really worked. That's what we don't want him to catch on to. That's why he's got to be blotted out before he does, some way or other. I haven't felt safe since Turner saw him sneaking around the south mouth of that infernal canyon. What was he lookin' for down there? He's as smart as he's salty, don't forget that, and plenty of both. He's got to be shoved out of the way.'

'Well, why not shove him out?' growled the hand who had wanted to know about Hatfield.

Morton gave him a look of disgust. 'Twice it's been tried, and we failed both times. If you could shoot as fast as you can gab, Watts, you'd have done for him down there in the canyon.'

'How in blazes was I to know he's got eyes that can see through a tree trunk?' demanded the cowhand, angrily. 'I still can't see how he spotted me. I was holed up for fair, but he saw me, and slid out of the hull just as I pulled trigger. Up went his horse, and took the slug, and gave him somethin' to take cover behind. And who the devil would have thought of that rifle barrel trick he used to come through the brush fire! Sometimes I think he ain't human!'

'Tell you what,' suggested another hard-faced individual, 'I'll pick a row with him, make it look plumb legitimate, and down him.'

'*You* down *him!*' Morton snorted derisively. 'He'd take time to roll a cigarette first and still beat you to the draw! Be sure you have the sight filed off your gun before you reach. It won't hurt half so bad when he shoves it down your neck!'

The puncher swore angrily, but did not argue.

'We'll get the roundup over first,' Morton repeated. 'Everybody will be too busy workin' while that's goin' on to start anything. That is unless we can manage to get Skelton and Rawlins together for a showdown somewhere out on the range. After the roundup work is done, we'll make a move. I've got something planned that will give certain gents a surprise.'

Three days after that, without any untoward incident marking the interim, the big roundup got under way. Sheriff Dwyer had been doing some industrious spade work, meanwhile, the result of which was immediately apparent. When the ranch owners of the section met to discuss the details of the cow hunt, Raines Skelton proposed that Jim Hatfield be made roundup boss. No objection was raised, even Bert Rawlins agreeing with the man he considered his enemy, in this important matter.

When Hatfield was notified of his appointment, he understood perfectly Sheriff Dwyer's little scheme, and permitted himself a chuckle.

'That old-timer has plenty wrinkles on his horns,' he apostrophized the canny peace officer.

The truth of which was easily apparent. The roundup captain was always boss of the roundup in the strictest sense. His word was absolute law, no matter if he didn't own a hoof. The owners of the cows were as much under his orders as any puncher or horse wrangler. His commands were unquestioned and admitted of no argument. His disposition of the riders was final, and all differences of opinion were submitted to him for settlement, and from his decision there was no appeal. It was an unwritten law of the range and backed up to the letter by all concerned. Usually, also, the range boss was a man capable of backing up his judgment himself, without any assistance from others.

In this particular instance, nobody labored under any delusions as to the ability of the range boss to handle things. Owners and hands who had never seen Hatfield regarded with curiosity, interest and respect the man who had jailed the Forked S and run the Bradded R out of town.

'I'm not surprised,' said one grizzled old rancher. 'Look at his eyes. How'd you like to see 'em turned in your direction over the sights of a six-gauge?'

Hatfield's first act, after selecting the hands he decided upon to serve as lieutenants in command of the various groups, was to assign riders to the terrains they would work over. As a result, Raines Skelton and his Forked S hands invariably found themselves at one end of the section, while the Bradded Rs were at the other and miles away.

There was no chance for the two outfits to get together, singly or as a whole, except at the holding spot, and no outfit would think of starting trouble at the holding spot, no matter how strong the inclination. To do so would mean to find every man's hand against them. The holding spot was altogether too important a place to permit the luxury of private feuds.

CHAPTER TWELVE

ROUNDUP DAYS

Lucky Seven, old Tolliver Truxton's spread, east of the Bradded R. and centrally located, had been designated as the main holding spot and here the collected cows were held in close herd. The troops of cowboys under the designated leaders rode out over the range. Soon these groups broke up into small parties or single units until the hands were separated by distances that varied with the topography of the country.

Each man's duty was to hunt out all the cattle on the ground over which he rode, carefully searching for scattered individual animals or small bunches. These were gathered together and driven to the holding spot. As the herd grew, the riders changed horses and invaded the concentrated mass of cattle. The horses now were especially trained cutting horses and knew their business as well as did their riders. The cutting out would begin, calling for skillful and bold horsemanship and involving considerable personal danger.

The cows wanted were divorced from the main herd and driven before the tally man. Then, as indicated by their brands, they were distributed to the various subsidiary holding spots which were the individual corrals that belonged to the several ranches participating in the roundup.

Here again there was cutting. Cattle wanted for shipping were cut out. The culls and the cutbacks were allowed to roam once more. After being properly classified, they were driven to their home range and turned loose. The beef cut was held in close formation.

Calves were branded in accordance with the brand worn by their mothers. Out would flash a hissing rope. A startled bawl of the calf. The rope hums taut as the trained horse takes up the slack. The calf is dragged to the fire where the various branding irons are heating. The rider leathers his way along the taut rope to the jumping, bawling calf.

'Bradded R!' he shouts.

'Bradded R!' repeats the tally man, writing it down in his book.

The cowboy catches the calf under the flank and by the neck. Over it goes, with a bleat of terror. Another hand runs forward and grips a leg. The glowing iron comes out of the fire. There is a crisping and sizzling, the acrid smell of scorched hair. A bawl from the calf, another bawl as its ears are notched.

Off comes the rope. The calf scrambles to its feet and bleats its way toward its anxious and angry mother, who has been fended away from the scene of operations. The cow licks the wound and the calf quickly forgets all about its unpleasant experience.

With the instinct of the born cattleman, Jim Hatfield loved the roundup. The dust, the heat, the sweat, the shouting and the tumult of hectic activity. The day began with the jangling *br-r-r-r-!* of the cook's little nickel plated alarm clock at four in the morning. It ended when the lovely blue dusk sifted down like an impalpable dust from the surrounding hills.

In the blaze of the noonday sun, under the stars of night the work went on in one phase or another. In deference to the turbulent condition of the range, Hatfield refrained from night drives, consisting of small squads of hands sent out ten or fifteen miles from the chuck-wagons to camp on their own hook and early in the morning begin driving cattle in the country designated for the next day's working.

'We'll hold 'em here where we can keep an eye on 'em after dark,' he told the spread owners. There was no argument.

So after the sun had set and the moon soared up in the west, the only sounds of activity were the singing of the night hawks and the steady clump of their horses' irons as they rode ceaselessly around the bunched and sleeping cattle.

And all the while, Hatfield was pondering the problem upon which he felt sure the future of peace or bloody war for the Mist River range depended. The problem for which he must find a solution, which centered about mysterious Mist River Canyon.

'If I can figure that one out, I'm fairly sure the rest will be easy,' he told himself. 'I've got to get a look into that canyon, somehow or other.'

The problem was far from easy of solution. To attempt to ride up the canyon from the south mouth, where the water was shallow, was out of the question. No horse could stand the battering of the current for long.

To enter the canyon from the north would be to gamble his life on the theory he had evolved during hours of painful thinking under the stars. The risk was too great to take save as a final desperate chance when all else had failed.

For Hatfield had a theory, a startling and unusual theory that had had its inception in his belief that there was less water in Mist River south of the canyon than there was to the north. If his surmise was correct, he was up against the most novel form of cow stealing he had ever encountered.

'I've seen some good ones, but if I'm right about this one, it's in a class by itself and darn near foolproof,' he declared to himself as he lay watching the great clock in the sky wheel westward before the advance of the dawn.

The roundup ended with a careful combing of the brakes and canyons for strays.

'I don't want any hiding cows left behind,' Hatfield warned his men. 'And there won't be unless there's some bad or careless combing. Get going, now. I'm riding your trail.'

The spread owners were elated by the results.

'The best roundup we ever had,' they declared to a man. 'Morton, you don't want to let that fellow Hatfield get away from you. If you do, one of us will snap him up so fast it'll make your head swim. You don't come on a range boss like him once in a year of Sundays.'

'He is sort of out of the ordinary,' Morton agreed, a slight touch of grimness in his voice.

Finally all was finished. Each outfit trailed its beef herd and headed for home. As all outfits on this range had participated in the roundup, there were no drifts—cows belonging to spreads not taking part in the roundup that had wandered onto the roundup range—to be cut out and shoved onto their home range.

Once the beef herds were on their home grounds, they were held close, against the time for taking the trail to the various shipping points. The punchers, except those unfortunates who had been chosen by lot to look after the herds, headed for Crater and a celebration.

Hatfield did not ride with the hands. After conferring with the various spread owners and checking figures, he rode in the general direction of Crater, just as dusk was falling. Before reaching the town, however, he veered to the south.

Moonrise found him at the base of the Mist River Hills and only a short distance south of the north mouth of the canyon. Lounging comfortably in the saddle, one leg hooked over the horn, he rolled and lighted a cigarette and smoked thoughtfully, contemplating the rugged slopes swelling upward into the moon-drenched sky.

He pinched out his cigarette butt and searched about until he found a small clearing surrounded by growth. A thread of water ran across the clearing which was grass-grown. He got the rig off Goldy, stored saddle and bridle beneath a bush and turned the sorrel loose to graze. He removed his rope from the saddle and looped it over his shoulder. Then with a last glance around, and confident his well-trained horse would not stray, he headed for the hill slopes.

What Hatfield proposed to do would have been bad enough in the daytime, but with the added handicap of the deceptive moonlight, it bordered on stark, staring lunacy.

Nevertheless, he tackled the slopes, working his way upward by the most practicable routes he could find.

The first two-thirds of the climb was not so bad, although there were places to make a man's hair bristle. But from then on the going was frightfully hazardous, with Hatfield clinging with fingers and toes to tiny cracks and ledges in the jagged wall.

Progress was of the snail-pace variety and infinitely tiring. Every crevice and blotch and mottling of the cliff face remained indelibly stamped on his memory. Time after time it seemed he had reached an impasse, with further advance impossible. But each time he managed to search out a way, with the risk of certain death constantly present, by which he could negotiate a few more feet of the towering battlement.

Hours passed, and at last he reached a point some thirty feet below the rimrock, from which further ascent seemed utterly out of the question. The cliff face was absolutely smooth, unbroken by rift or crevice, unscarred by ledges. Clinging to some knobs of stone, his feet resting on a narrow ledge, he considered the situation, studying the rimrock above.

His gaze centered on a projecting spur of stone. It was perhaps a foot in diameter and some two feet in length and jutted out horizontally from the lip of the cliff.

'Maybe it can be done,' he muttered, and unloosed the rope from around his shoulders. He built a loop, began twirling the rope.

It was an almost impossible stance from

which to make an upward cast, utterly impossible for a roper with less than the Lone Wolf's ability. But when Hatfield's arm flipped the loop it spiraled gracefully into the air and noosed the projecting fang of stone. He drew the rope through the honda, tightening the loop, and tested it as best he could for security and strength.

The spur seemed firm enough, but if it happened to be loose where the base joined the parent rock, well, there were five hundred feet of nothingness beneath him, with the jagged crags below thrusting upward like the teeth of a giant trap.

Drawing a deep breath, Hatfield trusted his weight to the rope. He swung out from the cliff face, with the awful depths yawning up toward him, and the moon-fired rim above seeming a long way off.

Tensing his tired muscles, Hatfield began the terrible climb. Foot by torturous foot, he dragged his body upward, his fingers gripping the smooth, hard, seven-sixteenths manila that was never intended for rope climbing by moonlight. Once he heard a slight crackling sound above, and set his teeth. If the spur was loosening from the cliff face, he had but a short time to live.

But the sound was either a figment of overwrought imagination or a slight shifting of the loop. The rock held and in another minute he was clambering over the jagged rim to sprawl exhausted on the flat surface of the cliff crest.

After a while he sat up and gazed about. The view was magnificent. To the east rolled the rangeland, the bristles of thickets, the groves and the level pastures silvered and softened by the moonshine. The mountains to the west were a purple mystery etched and bordered by ash and chrome, their crests crowned in pale flame. To the south he could view the gray desolation of the desert, appearing as strange and alien to man as the star-studded sky above. To the north the black rim of the cliffs stood out dark and ominous, with a void of eternity beyond.

Hatfield got to his feet and headed west across the cliff crest. It was jagged and broken, pitted with holes and crevices, but negotiable even in the uncertain light. A quarter of a mile of laborious walking found him on the dizzy lip of Mist River Canyon.

The moon was directly overhead, but he could see no great distance into the depths because of the swirling, rolling fog that veiled the waters and gave the river its name. He sat down, his back against a lump of stone, rolled and lighted a cigarette and awaited the dawn.

At last it came, scarlet and rose and tremulous gold. A bird winged its way through the crystal immensities, its liquid note drifting down to where Hatfield sat, a thin, pulsing thread of exquisite melody. The flaming rim of the sun appeared and light poured over the mountain tops in a flood.

But it took some time for the sun warmth to dissipate the mists in the canyon's depths. Hatfield turned and gazed north. In the strengthening light he noted something that quickened his pulses.

The north mouth of the canyon was no great distance off. He could see that the mouth of the canyon was cramped. Little more than a hundred yards south of where the river entered the canyon, the gorge opened out abruptly to full twice its previous width. Hatfield's eyes glowed as he gazed at the unusual formation.

'Looks like my hunch might be a straight one,' he remarked aloud exultantly. 'We'll soon find out.'

He turned and peered over the lip. The mists were gone now and he could glimpse, more than a thousand feet below, the white and silver streak that was Mist River, foaming over its rocky bed.

The descent to the water's surface looked hard, but not nearly so bad as the cliff face he had been forced to negotiate to reach the rim. The canyon wall, which was not perpendicular but had a slight outward slant, was cracked and fissured and jutted with ledges.

CHAPTER THIRTEEN

THE CANYON SECRET

Glancing at the sun, Hatfield tightened his belt and started down. In little more than an hour his feet touched a narrow strip of sandy beach that bordered the stream. He rested for a while, then boldly entered the river. With another thrill of exultation, he found that the water, even in mid-river, came no more than halfway up his thighs. He turned upstream and sloshed along until he was close to where the river poured in a foaming torrent through the cramped mouth of the canyon to spread out over the greater width of the lower canyon and quickly lose depth and power of current.

'So far so good,' Hatfield muttered. 'Cows tumbled into the water north of the canyon wouldn't drown before they were swept through the cramped mouth. They'd take a beating, but they'd still be all right when they hit the shallow water down here. The question is, now, does the canyon remain the same all the way to the south mouth, or does it cramp again? If it does for any distance, my hunch is strictly off-trail. It it doesn't, I'm riding straight, and certain gents are in for a surprise they won't relish. That's something more for me to find out.'

He climbed back onto the narrow strip of beach and proceeded down-canyon, eyeing the cracked and seamed sides of the gorge with interest.

The sandy beach was not continuous. At times he was sloshing through shallow water. A manifestation he encountered now and then interested him greatly. Opposite some of the cracks in the wall, the water was deeper than usual, and here swirls and eddies plucked at his legs. He nodded with satisfaction after several such experiences.

'No wonder there's less water down toward the south than there is toward the north,' he chuckled. 'Some of those cracks are drains into underground caverns. The water keeps escaping by way of them, and shrinking the river. That's why it keeps getting shallower all the time.'

It took time to cover the more than seven miles to the south mouth of the gorge, although the increasing frequency of the stretches of beach made the going comparatively easy. It was past noon when Hatfield finally sloshed out of the stream and sat down on the bank to rest and dry off. Nowhere had he encountered deep water or hard going.

'Cows would amble all the way down without more than getting their legs wet,' he told himself. 'They'd keep on going until they got out, of course, with nothing to eat in there.

Well, this sort of clears things up. A smooth scheme if I ever heard of one. About the only way to get the critters out of the country, the way the land lies hereabouts, but with them once down here on the desert, to shove 'em on to Mexico, or anywhere else, is simple. Now if I can just out-fox a few gents, things should work out fine.'

In a complacent frame of mind, he set out on the long trudge back to the thicket where he had left Goldy.

Just as the sun was setting in a sky of saffron flame, he got the rig on the sorrel and headed for town.

Hatfield found the sheriff in his office. Doc Cooper was also present.

'Got an answer to your wire to Captain McDowell,' said Dwyer, and handed it to him.

Hatfield took the message, and read:

THE BOWERS BROTHERS, JOSEPH AND WILLIAM, RETURNED TO THEIR HOME NEAR CHOLA DOWN IN THE BEND WHEN THEY WERE RELEASED FROM JAIL. GOT MIXED UP IN A SHOOTING THERE A FEW MONTHS LATER AND TOOK IT ON THE RUN, PRESUMABLY TO MEXICO. NO FURTHER TRACE OF THEM. NO LINE ON THE OTHERS. DROPPED OUT OF SIGHT AS SOON AS THEY LEFT THE PRISON.

Hatfield folded the telegram and placed it in his pocket.

'Not much, but something,' he commented. 'It would seem, from the way the Bowers boys headed back home as soon as they were released that they prefer to work in familiar territory. Chola is no great distance from here, and it is not illogical that they should show up around here. Things are beginning to tie up, and maybe we'll have our chance to drop a loop before long. We'll try and make the chance, anyhow. I'm so worn out now, though, that I'm going to have something to eat and go to bed. But tomorrow, Sheriff, you and I will ride over to the Bradded R and have a talk with Bert Rawlins.'

Hatfield and Dwyer headed for the Bradded R early the following morning. Bert Rawlins' heavy brows knit as he watched them ride up his wagon road.

'Something in the wind,' he told his foreman. 'That pair are not coming here for nothing. Have any of the boys been actin' up of late?'

'Not that I know of,' the foreman assured him.

'Well, we'll soon find out,' Rawlins predicted. 'Wish I knew just what they want. When that big hombre there shows up, somebody is usually due for a surprise.'

The foreman nodded. 'Chances are they just want a palaver with you,' he remarked. 'I'm goin' to make myself scarce. Give a whoop if you want me. I'll be out in the yard.'

The Bradded R owner was in for a surprise, all right, but something different from anything he expected. He ushered his visitors into his big living room and sat down with them. He glanced questioningly at the sheriff.

'Want to have a little talk with you, Bert,' said Dwyer.

'I'm listenin',' Rawlins replied. 'Shoot.'

Hatfield was fumbling with a cunningly concealed secret pocket in his broad leather belt. He laid something on the table beside the ranch owner.

Bert Rawlins stared, his jaw sagging. The object was a gleaming silver star set on a silver circle, the feared and honored badge of the Texas Rangers.

Rawlins raised his eyes to Hatfield's face. He shook his red head.

'I might have known it,' he said. 'I should have known it from the start. You act like a Ranger.'

'Bert, you're talkin' to the Lone Wolf,' Sheriff Dwyer said, proudly.

Rawlins' eyes opened still wider as he stared at the almost legendary figure whose exploits were the talk of the Southwest.

'I might have known that, too,' he declared. 'Nobody else could have done the things you've been doin' hereabouts of late. The Lone Wolf! Well, what's up? Am I headed for the calaboose?'

'Chances are you ought to be,' grunted the

sheriff, 'but not yet, I reckon. Hatfield has a little scheme cooked up he wants you to give us a hand with.'

'Shoot,' repeated Rawlins, 'I'm listenin'.'

As Hatfield talked, Rawlins' face mirrored incredulous amazement.

'If anybody else was tellin' me that, I wouldn't believe a word of it,' he declared. 'Of all the damned things I ever heard of! No, I never would have believed it.'

He shook his head, frowned, muttered a few highly expressive words. But as Hatfield further unfolded his plan, Rawlins began to grin. Finally he leaned back in his chair and roared with laughter.

'I'll do it!' he chuckled. 'That's one thing me and the boys can do without much coachin'.'

'Don't do it too well,' Hatfield warned, as he smiled.

'We won't,' Rawlins replied. 'We'll do it just right, but I'll bet we fool anybody who might try keepin' tabs on us.'

'Fooling that bunch isn't as easy as it sounds,' Hatfield warned again, this time a trifle grimly. 'They've got plenty experience behind them, and a wary lot.'

'Leave it to me,' Rawlins assured him. 'I'm askin' only one thing, to be in on the shindig when it starts.'

'I suppose you've got that coming to you,' Hatfield agreed as he rose to his feet. 'Now, I'd better be getting back to the Bar M. They'll

122

begin to wonder down there what's become of me. I'm due to make a check on the south range some time today.'

'Most of the boys are driftin' back to their spreads,' remarked the sheriff, 'with empty pockets and sore heads, but they had a good time and don't mind much. I'll head up to the Forked S and put a bug in Raines Skelton's ear, so he won't get the wrong notion and do somethin' to tangle the twine.'

Bert Rawlins met the sheriff's eyes squarely. 'And while you're at it, you might tell him I said I'm sorry,' he suggested.

Hatfield smiled. 'I've an idea,' he said, 'this is going to be a pretty nice range for a working cowboy to coil his twine in.'

'And I've got a good idea who'll be responsible,' Rawlins declared with emphasis.

The next day, about mid-morning, Sheriff Dwyer and his four deputies rode north toward the town of Foster.

'Labor trouble in the railroad yards up there,' the sheriff explained as he left his office in charge of a clerk.

Citizens of Crater were convinced that the sheriff should have allowed the railroad workers to solve their own problems when, shortly before noon, the Bradded R outfit, all but three hands who had been left to guard the big shipping herd, and including Bert Rawlins, boomed into town in a decidedly belligerent mood. They took over the Last Chance Saloon and started an uproarious session of drinking and poker.

'Nobody's runnin' us out of town this time!' declared Rawlins. 'Let somebody try it, including that cussed Skelton and his bunch of cow-runnin' no-goods!'

Soon the town of Crater was in a decidedly jittery condition. The Bradded Rs were drinking heavily and getting uglier by the hour. Punchers from other outfits drifted into town, looked the situation over, and quietly drifted out again. They wanted no part of what appeared to be the beginning of a bloody climax to the Mist River range feud.

Among the cowboys in town were several of Pres Morton's Bar M bunch, including his foreman, a lanky, taciturn individual who claimed to have hailed originally from Arizona, but was always rather vague as to his antecedents. The keen-eyed Rawlins noted that the foreman wore a slightly amused, and decidedly pleased expression as he looked over the antics of the celebrating Bradded R hands.

As the afternoon and evening wore on, the Bradded Rs scattered out from time to time, by ones and twos, ambling around to give the other saloons and places a once-over, but always ending up at the Last Chance again, where the main body of the outfit kept close together.

Meanwhile, down on the Bradded R range, the three hands guarding the shipping herd appeared to be having a little celebration of their own. A bottle passed from hand to hand with increasing frequency. Soon song was disturbing the peace of the rangeland, song that should have discomposed the nerves of the bunched cows rather than soothe them.

The beefs, however, with peculiar tastes as to music, apparently didn't resent the raucous bellowings, and settled down to placid contentment as the shades of evening lengthened, and the stars began weaving their web of silver across the darkening sky. The three punchers, after a period of noisy wrangling, curled up in their blankets beside a dying fire and soon were snoring.

In Crater, the noisy and combative Bradded Rs still kept drifting in and out of the Last Chance. The poker game had been roaring for hours and an astonishing amount of whiskey had passed across the bar to the two large tables that had been placed end to end to accommodate the gamblers.

As darkness fell, Rawlins himself wandered out to look over the town. With rather unsteady steps he made his way from bar to bar, gradually working toward the quieter western part of Crater. Finally, when he was sure he was unobserved, he slid down a silent side street and with steps that had abruptly become surprisingly firm and purposeful headed for his horse, tied at a little used rack not far from an empty corral. In three minutes he was clear of the town and speeding across the prairie.

Near where the shipping herd was bedded down, a dense bristle of thicket showed in the starlight. Rawlins approached the thicket cautiously. He showed no surprise when shadowy figures loomed up on each side of his walking horse.

'It's all right,' he told Jim Hatfield. 'I'm plumb sure they fell for it. The show the boys are puttin' on is worth watchin'.'

'Hope they don't overdo it,' observed Sheriff Dwyer from the other side of the horse. 'A gabblin' drunk might give the whole thing away.'

'Don't worry,' Rawlins reassured him. 'The boys are copper-lined to begin with, and what nobody notices is that most of the liquor goes in the spittoons. Arn Hearn pulled a lulu. Arn ordered a quart for the table, and when nobody was lookin', he pocketed the bottle of red-eye and slid a bottle of cold tea on the table in place of it. Arn had two quarts of Chinese delight cached in his chaps.'

Sheriff Dwyer chuckled. 'Looks good, all right,' he admitted.

Hatfield glanced toward where the cows were grunting and grumbling in full-fed satisfaction.

'I believe it's going to work,' he said. 'That big herd of prime beefs, left unguarded that way, sure ought to be a temptation to any rustling outfit keeping an eye on things. It's pretty safe to assume that as soon as it got dark somebody was snooping around here looking things over. But I wish the showdown would come in a hurry. This waiting isn't easy on the nerves.'

He led Rawlins into the depths of the thicket, where Dwyer's four deputies, plus a half-dozen specials, and the three 'drunken' Bradded R punchers left to guard the herd were comfortably holed up.

'Might as well take it easy,' he told Rawlins. 'If they show, the first thing they'll do is throw lead into those blanket rolls there by the fire. That'll give us plenty of warning.'

CHAPTER FOURTEEN

THE TRAP

The thicket was ideal for an ambuscade. Over to one side was a little rise, upon which the shadowy outlines of the blanket rolls showed in a faint glow cast by the embers of the fire. Less than a hundred feet from the bristle of growth, the herd lay in drowsy peace. Anybody approaching the cattle would be plainly discernible in the shimmer of starlight.

In addition, at the edge of the thicket was a great bundle of oil-drenched brush ready to flare into flame at the touch of a match. The posse, in the shadows, would enjoy this advantage, which Hatfield had planned. All that could be done had been done. Now there was nothing to do but await the expected approach of the rustlers.

Slowly the hours passed. Midnight came and went as the stars wheeled westward. Another hour, and Hatfield began to grow decidedly uneasy. he experienced a disquieting feeling that all was not well.

'As I figure it, they should have been here before now, if they're coming at all,' he told Sheriff Dwyer. 'I don't think they'd risk shoving a herd across the range in daylight again. They came close to getting caught the last time they tried that, when Rawlins and his hands chased them into the hills. They'd sure have to step the herd along now to get the critters to the river before dawn. It's beginning to look as if my hunch wasn't as good as I thought it was. But I've still got an ace in the hole.'

The sheriff shook his head, and peered eastward.

'Maybe somethin' happened,' he hazarded.

Sheriff Dwyer was more right than he could have guessed. Something had happened. Was, in fact, happening at just about that time.

Old Tolliver Truxton's Lucky Seven was the best stocked spread in the section. Not so large as the Forked S, it was even better range and easier to work. Cupped against the eastern hills, it enjoyed an advantage of position that had so far rendered it immune to the depredations of the owlhoots.

Tolliver Truxton was a shrewd cowman. He went in for careful breeding and his beefs commanded the best prices the market afforded. Truxton had only one fault. He was pretty easy-going and complacent. He had held aloof from the feud that threatened to devastate the range, and felt that so long as he remained aloof, he would avoid trouble and losses. Up to the moment, his judgment had proved correct. Because of which he had been lulled into a false sense of security.

Tonight, his big shipping herd of prime beefs, which would take the trail on the morrow, was bedded down in a canyon mouth on his west pasture, where it would be most convenient to start the trek north to Foster. Three night hawks guarded the herd, and had little to do, for the night was warm and still, with a clear sky of glowing stars and no hint of wind or rain. The three punchers assigned to the night trick took it easy and paid little attention to what went on around them.

Because, so far as they could ascertain, there was nothing going on. That is, until just after midnight when the three grouped together, lounging comfortably in their saddles for a smoke and a gab.

Jess Ballard, one of the hands, let his

lighted cigarette slip through his fingers. The grass was tall and rather dry and a glowing butt was fraught with possibilities of trouble. With a grunt, Ballard swung over in his saddle to retrieve the fallen cigarette. To that simple incident of chance, he owed his life.

For even as Ballard swayed downward, from the dark canyon mouth burst a roar of gunfire!

Ballard's two companions went down without a sound. They never knew what hit them. Ballard also went down, shocked to paralysis by the smash of a heavy slug through his left shoulder. Helpless, all but senseless, he lay without sound or motion beside his dead bunkies. The dark figures swooping from the canyon mouth had no reason to believe that Ballard was not as thoroughly dead as his companions.

Ballard retained enough of consciousness to see and understand what happened next. Through a fog of pain and nausea, he watched the drygulchers lash the cattle to their feet and send them bleating and bawling in wild flight across the prairie. Before he was able to get to his feet, even move, the herd had vanished in the shadows to the west.

Sick, dizzy, half-crazed with suffering, Ballard finally managed to crawl to his horse, pull himself up by the stirrup straps and mount the nervous animal. He twisted his spurs into the stirrup leather, twined his fingers in the horse's coarse mane and sent it scudding for the ranchhouse more than two miles distant.

The banging of Ballard's gun aroused old Tol Truxton and the Lucky Seven punchers from their slumbers. Ballard slid from his saddle and half-crawled up the ranch-house steps. He was able to gasp out his story before he fainted from pain and loss of blood.

The cook went to work on Ballard. Truxton sent a man racing to Crater and the sheriff's office. He and the rest of his outfit roared westward on the trail of the owlhoots.

'The sidewinders will be headin' for the river, sure as shootin', curse 'em to the devil!' swore Truxton. 'If we don't catch up with 'em before they get there our cows will go where the others from hereabouts have been goin'. Sift sand, you jugheads! Sift sand!'

It wanted but two hours of dawn when the disgusted and irritable posse in the thicket heard the approach of fast hoofs.

'Somebody comin', and comin' fast,' said the sheriff. 'He's not tryin' to keep under cover, either. Golly, listen to him yelp!'

A moment later, Dwyer recognized the voice of the whooping rider.

'It's my clerk!' he exclaimed. 'What in blazes?' He raised his voice. 'Here, Porter, this way!'

The clerk crashed up to the thicket, slithered his horse to a stop and dropped from the hull. He panted out his story to an accompaniment of blistering oaths from his

131

hearers.

Jim Hatfield's face set in lines bleak as chiseled granite.

'Out-foxed, that's all,' he said quietly. 'We never fooled 'em a bit. They caught onto our little scheme without any trouble, made sure that we were all holed up here and then hit where least expected . . .' Well, here's where I play my ace. It'll take time for those cows to drift through the canyon. We've got a chance to hit the sidewinders down at the south mouth of the canyon before they collect the beefs and shove across the desert.' He looked questioningly at the clerk. 'You say it happened around midnight, Porter? All right, gents, fork your cayuses, we're riding.'

'Might have been best to land on 'em down there by the river, while they were waiting for the cows to come through, in the first place,' remarked Sheriff Dwyer as the posse got under way.

'It looks that way,' admitted Hatfield, 'but I'd hoped to bag them without a bad fight. Remember, Pres Morton and most of his owlhoot bunch have already had a taste of prison life. If they can help it, they'll not go back to serve the long sentences they would be sure to get as second offenders. They'll be desperate. This means a shooting, with little advantage on our side, unless I can think of something . . .' No, there's nothing else for it. I was outsmarted, that's all. I gave Morton credit for plenty of savvy, but he's got more than I imagined.'

'Nobody can figure out everything, especially when dealin' with that sort of snake-blooded outfit,' Sheriff Dwyer comforted the Ranger. 'Don't worry, we'll get 'em!'

In the dark hour before the dawn the posse stormed south across the star-burned prairie.

As they rode, Jim Hatfield did some hard thinking. With his uncanny memory for topographical details, he reconstructed in his mind the terrain that approached the south canyon mouth. He evolved a plan, a desperate plan that might well cost him his life, but which promised the capture of the owlhoots with the least possible risk to the men with the Ranger.

Mile after mile flowed under the horses' drumming irons. The false dawn fled like a pale ghost across the sky. A faint glow birthed in the east, slowly strengthened. The stars began to dwindle. A soft wind whispered out of the west.

As the posse rode in the shadow of the cliffs where the Mist River Hills ended, wan light was shimmering the desert.

Objects were taking form, their blurred edges sharpening. It wanted but little of sunrise when they sighted the bulge beyond which was the south mouth of Mist River Canyon.

'Take it easy, now,' Hatfield cautioned his men. 'Keep in the shadow under the cliffs and walk your horses, slow. If we can make it to that jut without being spotted, we've got a chance to put this over.'

At a snail's pace the posse closed in on the bulge. Back of the great fang of granite they drew rein. Nothing had happened, and Hatfield breathed easier. He listened intently and to his keen ears came, above the rush of the river, the sound of voices.

'They're there, all right,' he whispered to Sheriff Dwyer. 'Now I'm going to try and attract and hold their attention till you men can slide around the cliff. I'm going to ride straight south, fast, and curve around to hit them on a slant. That should draw their fire and give the rest of you a chance to land on them before they know what's going on.'

'Good glory, Hatfield!' Dwyer protested in a hoarse whisper. 'You're committin' suicide!'

'Maybe not,' Hatfield replied. 'Got to chance it, anyhow. If they hear us coming around the bulge, they'll be all set for us and knock us over like squattin' quail. This way we may bag 'em without losing too many men.'

He hesitated an instant, running his eye over the silent group. 'I could use one man with me,' he said, 'but I'm not ordering anybody to take the chance.' He held up his hand. 'No, Sheriff, not you. I want you here to lead the bunch.'

Bert Rawlins leaned forward, a determined look on his ugly face.

'I reckon I've got more interest in this shindig than anybody else here,' he said with a finality that brooked no argument. 'I'm ridin' with you, Hatfield. All set?'

Jim Hatfield gathered up his reins, loosened his guns in their sheaths. On his broad breast gleamed the silver star of the Rangers. His eyes were as coldly gray as frosted steel.

'Let's go,' he said, and touched Goldy with his knee.

The great sorrel raced forward. Close beside him drummed Bert Rawlins' big black.

They flickered past the ragged jut of the cliffs, sped southward, swerved to the west as a chorus of yells and curses whirled up from the river bank.

'In the name of the State of Texas!' Hatfield thundered. 'You are under arrest!'

Running about in wild confusion were nearly a dozen men. Hatfield sighted Pres Morton, his face convulsed with rage and apprehension, bellowing orders. Guns boomed. Lead hissed around the advancing pair.

But Goldy had gone into a weaving, flickering dance that made him and his rider about as elusive a target as a glancing sunbeam. Rawlins' black hadn't been trained to such antics when under fire, but the thunder of the guns convulsed him with a terror that was evinced in a paroxysm of sunfishing and walking-beaming that was almost as effective as Goldy's dance.

Hatfield's guns were streaming fire and Rawlins was blazing away as best he could from the back of his end-swapping horse.

And with the turmoil at its frenzied height, around the bulge roared Sheriff Dwyer and his posse.

Caught between two fires, utterly unprepared for this latest unexpected development, the owlhoots broke in panic. Shooting, howling, they ducked and dodged. Half a dozen were down already.

They emptied two saddles as the posse charged, then scattered in every direction.

Hatfield and Rawlins charged toward them, veering their horses to get the possemen out of line. As they dived into the yelling, cursing, shooting tangle, Hatfield saw a lone horseman flash past at the river's brink. He recognized Pres Morton mounted on his superb roan. He jerked Goldy around, but before he could free himself of the pandemonium that raged all around him, Morton had a good half-mile lead.

A quick glance told Hatfield that Sheriff Dwyer had the situation here well in hand.

'I'll get Morton!' he shouted to the sheriff, and sent his sorrel racing in pursuit.

'Trail, Goldy, trail!' he urged.

CHAPTER FIFTEEN

LAST PLAY OF A RUSTLER

Extending himself instantly, the golden horse was off. His ears flattened back, he slugged his head about the bit. His steely legs shot backward like pistons as he fairly poured his long body over the ground. Eyes rolling, nostrils flaring red, he thundered after the flying roan.

But in the tall roan, Goldy had nearly met his match, and besides Goldy had already done ten fast miles without a pause for rest. He closed the distance, but slowly, slowly.

Hatfield settled himself in the saddle for a long and hard chase.

'If that owlhoot makes the Rio Grande and gets across, he's mighty liable to give me the slip,' he told himself.

Mile after mile flickered past. The flying hoofs drummed up the dawn and the lifted irons glinted with the first rays of the rising sun.

And, peering ahead, Hatfield saw what was likely to be more effective in Morton's favor than the speed and endurance of his gallant horse. Less than two miles ahead, a wavering, shifting curtain had magically risen from the desert's face, an opaque curtain, constantly changing form.

Hatfield well knew what the mysterious appearing curtain was. The wind had risen with the dawn, blowing sharply from the west. Down there it was at gale force and was lifting the loose particles in a blinding sand storm.

'If he gets into that far enough ahead, we'll lose him sure as shooting!' he muttered grimly. 'Trail, Goldy, trail!'

Goldy gave his best. Yard by straining yard, he closed the distance.

The dust storm was spreading out as it roared eastward. Morton reached its writhing fringe, was swallowed up in a mist of flying particles. But Goldy was close behind him now, and Hatfield could still dimly make out his form through the curdling yellow shadows. He loosened his guns in their sheaths, leaned forward in the saddle.

Morton glanced back, saw that he could not hope to outrun the speeding golden horse. He jerked his roan to a halt, whirled him about and drew his gun. Fire streamed from its muzzle. The reports echoed back hollowly from the sand clouds.

Hatfield answered the owlhoot's fire, shot for shot. It was a weird battle of shadows blasting death at each other through the swirling yellow murk.

But it was almost blind shooting. Lead hissed past Hatfield's face. A bullet burned a red streak along his bronzed cheek. Another turned his hat sideward on his head. He blazed away at Morton with the guns in both hands, but the widelooper still sat his horse.

Hatfield heard his hammers click on empty shells. There was no time to reload. Straight at Morton's flaming gun he charged.

A slug tore through the flesh of his upper arm and knocked him sideward with the shock. He recovered his balance just as Goldy hit the roan shoulder to shoulder.

Down went the roan! And down went Goldy on top of him. Hatfield and Morton were flung to the sand together.

Morton stabbed his gun forward and fired. The powder flame seared Hatfield's cheek. Then fingers of steel closed on Morton's wrist and doubled it back just as he pulled trigger again.

Morton gave a choking cry and slumped sideward. A hot flood gushed over Hatfield's hand as Morton's soul whimpered out between his blood-frothing lips and was gone.

Morton had shot himself through the throat.

Unsteadily, Hatfield got to his feet. He gazed down at the dead outlaw for a moment, then turned and stumbled to where his panting horse stood. He ripped away his sleeve, managed to fumble the roll of bandage from his saddle pouch and bind up his blood-gushing arm.

But the blood continued to flow freely,

dyeing the bandage scarlet, dripping from his fingers and sapping his strength.

With a mighty effort, he forked Goldy, turned his head north and sent him slogging through the roaring storm.

Swaying in the saddle, gripping the horn for support, Hatfield wondered dully if he would be able to make it out of the storm before he lost consciousness. Or would his bones whiten under the shifting sands, to keep cold company with Pres Morton's until the end of time?

Almost spent, Goldy shambled wearily on. Hatfield sagged lower and lower in the saddle, his eyes dull, his face drawn and haggard.

Suddenly, however, he raised his listless head. Somewhere ahead, shots were sounding. With trembling fingers he loaded one of his guns and fired answering signals. Shouts drifted toward him, drawing steadily nearer. Another moment and Sheriff Dwyer and Bert Rawlins burst through the murk.

'Did you get him?' the sheriff shouted as they ranged alongside.

'He sort of got himself,' Hatfield replied. 'Reckon the sand will have covered him up by now.'

He reeled, and would have fallen but for Rawlins' strong arm about his shoulders.

Hatfield remembered little about the ride back to Crater, but after Doc Cooper's skillful ministrations and a long sleep he felt fit for anything despite his stiff and sore arm and a sense of weariness.

'Just a tear,' Doc Cooper assured him. 'The slug made a clean hole and kept on going. Lucky it missed the bone. You won't notice it, except for the scar, in a couple of weeks. You lost considerable blood, though. That's why you feel tired.'

Hatfield learned from the sheriff that six of the outlaws had been killed and three captured. Three possemen had been wounded, two severely, but were expected to recover.

'The cows were stragglin' through and amblin' back to the grassland when we left,' Dwyer added. 'I sent word to Truxton to come down and get 'em. Rawlins set his boys to roundin' 'em up. Let's go over to the Deuces Up and eat. Rawlins is there, and Slade Gumbert and Raines Skelton. They all want to hear you tell about how you dropped your loop on Morton.'

A good breakfast brought Hatfield back to something like normal. Over the blue trickle of his cigarette smoke, he smiled at his expectant companions.

'Gumbert, you were the man I first had my eyes on,' he told the saloonkeeper. 'You see, I'd spotted you right off for a Mississippi River gambler on the run. I was sure you had worked on the river boats, and I was also sure you had got into serious trouble because of your card playing.'

'Why?' asked the sheriff.

'Because he didn't play any more,' Hatfield replied. 'A man who makes his living at cards doesn't stop playing except for a mighty good reason. I knew something had happened that had turned Gumbert from cards. Because it created in him an aversion to the game, and also because he wished to conceal his identity or past. Yes, I had my eye on Gumbert from the start, especially after I was sure he recognized me for a Ranger.'

'After I saw you in action once, down around Laredo, I was not apt to forget you,' Gumbert grunted.

Hatfield nodded, and paused to roll another cigarette.

'But Gumbert didn't fit into the picture just right,' he resumed when he had it lighted. 'From the way that bunch gave Rawlins and his men the slip in the hills when they widelooped his herd the day I hit the range, I felt sure that the man running things knew the country mighty well. A lot better than Gumbert could have possibly learned it during the time he had been here.

'Gumbert looked a natural that night when he came in covered with desert dust, but so did Pres Morton. He came in showing signs of hard riding that night, too. And, unlike Gumbert, he made no mention of where he had been. When I learned his holdings were north of the desert country I knew there was no good reason why he should have been riding around down there. Of course, all that didn't mean much, at first, especially not until I had given Gumbert a straight brand.'

'After you talked to me the day you were marshal of Crater,' Gumbert observed.

'Yes,' Hatfield replied, 'the day Morton lured the sheriff out of town by reporting a widelooping that never took place, aiming to set the stage for the showdown between the Forked S and the Bradded R. Another time Morton slipped, because I figured that one out in a hurry. That's why I went to work for Morton.'

'Taking the chance of gettin' yourself done in, at the same time,' interpolated the sheriff. 'Squattin' down in a nest of sidewinders! Fire and blazes!'

Hatfield smiled, and went on talking to Gumbert.

'I wanted to decide about you one way or the other, so I put the thing up to you squarely. You came clean with your story, and I saw you had made up your mind to find out, once and for all, if you were wanted in Texas. When I let you know, sort of off-trail, but in a way you understood, that you were not, you looked like another man. A gent riding a crooked trail doesn't confess to past trouble. An honest man often does, wanting to get it off his chest, pay up, if necessary, and then start over. I blotted your brand off my tally sheet after that talk.'

'Tell me,' interrupted Gumbert, 'how in

143

blazes did you know I used to work on the boats?'

'You whistle,' Hatfield said and smiled.

'Whistle!'

'That's right, and you whistle the chants and songs of the colored folks working the levees and the docks of the Big River. I never heard them any place else, certainly not in west Texas.'

Gumbert shook his head in admiration.

'How did you get a line on Morton?' asked the sheriff.

'Process of elimination,' the Ranger explained. 'With Gumbert crossed off, Morton became the logical suspect. Morton, born and reared in this part of the country and naturally familiar with it. Morton, who had dropped out of sight for a number of years and then come back with a vague story of wandering over various states. When we found Bob Hawley's body hanged beside Clem Buster's that morning, I was convinced that somebody was playing the old game of getting two outfits on the prod against each other to cover up his own depredations. Morton made his first bad mistake when he used two sections of the same old peculiarly braided tie rope to hang both bodies. To my mind that immediately cleared both the Forked S and the Bradded R. It was inconceivable that both outfits would own a section of that rope.'

'Clear enough,' commented Raines Skelton.

144

'Yes, the owlhoot brand always slip up on the little things,' Hatfield said. 'Morton slipped badly again when he cleared that canyon of cows before he had me trapped in there and tried to burn me up. There were plenty of cows in that gorge just a few days before. Morton didn't want to lose 'em, so he cleaned 'em out the night before the day he knew I aimed to work the canyon. Keeping all his new riders at the ranchhouse with him was also something to think about. He kept the men he had hired and his uncle's old riders separated. And he shoved Billy Wagner and myself into the bunkhouse with the old hands.'

'Those five who served time with him didn't work on the spread?' asked the sheriff.

'No,' Hatfield smiled. 'The Bowers brothers were wanted, and so were the others, we're likely to find out. They had been holed up somewhere else and Morton sent for them when he wanted to pull something out of the ordinary, like the attempted robbery at the Terlingua Mine. Morton, of course, was Peter Morrow, the safe cracker. Note the similarity of names. Owlhoots often pick aliases sounding like their own names.

'But Morton's first bad slip was his cleverest move. Running the cows through Mist River Canyon to the desert country was mighty clever, but it was the thing that first convinced me that somebody was deliberately setting two outfits against one another. It didn't make

145

sense to think Skelton and Rawlins were doing such things just to make trouble for each other. And when that sort of thing kept up, I got mighty curious about that canyon. Somebody was taking too many chances unless they had considerable to gain.

'It began to look as if those valuable cows weren't just feeding the fishes. So I looked over the south mouth of the canyon, saw that the water was shallow down there because of the greater width of the canyon, and got to wondering how far up that shallow water continued. Also I saw no drowned cows anywhere down there, which was peculiar, I thought. So I managed to get a look at the canyon farther up, and it became simple. All I had to do was drop a loop on Morton.'

'Uh-huh, that was all,' Sheriff Dwyer remarked drily. 'Well, you dropped it, all right, and we've got peace on this range once more.'

'And we're going to keep it, eh, Rawlins?' Raines Skelton declared vigorously. Rawlins said nothing, but his big hand stretched out to clasp the old rancher's.

Jim Hatfield stood up, smiling down at them.

'Well, I'll be riding,' he said. 'Captain Bill will have another little chore lined up for me by the time I get back to the Post. *Adios!*'

They watched him ride away, tall and graceful atop his golden horse. 'Gents,' said

Bert Rawlins, 'There goes a Ranger we owe more'n we can pay.'

We hope you have enjoyed this Large Print book. Other Chivers Press or G.K. Hall & Co. Large Print books are available at your library or directly from the publishers.

For more information about current and forthcoming titles, please call or write, without obligation, to:

Chivers Press Limited
Windsor Bridge Road
Bath BA2 3AX
England
Tel. (01225) 335336

OR

G.K. Hall & Co.
P.O. Box 159
Thorndike, Maine 04986
USA
Tel. (800) 223-2336

All our Large Print titles are designed for easy reading, and all our books are made to last.